Go Gently
The Cornwall Adventures Book 3

By
Nancy M Bell

ISBN: 978-1-77145-392-9

Publisher
Books We Love Ltd.
Chestermere, Alberta, Canada

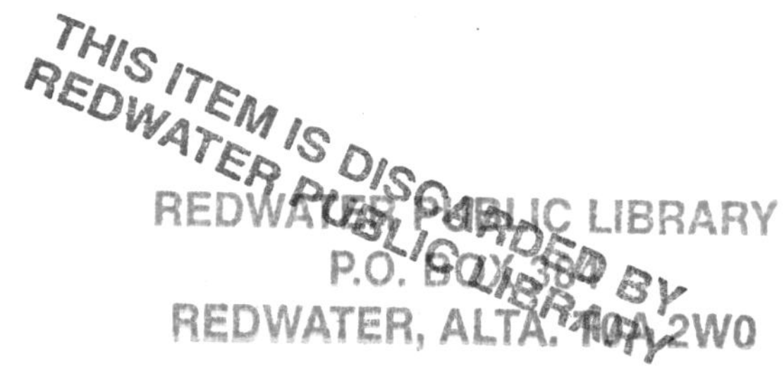

Dedication:

To all those who believe in magic and the power of love. Thanks to my friends in Cornwall who are never too busy to answer my questions.

To Sara, my friend and fellow author, who cheered me on during the writing of this book.

The invocation Sarie uses in the Teinmlaida is by Tira Brandan-Evans, an adaptation of The Lorica, better known as St. Patrick's Breastplate, and is used with her permission.

The words for Tom Bawcock's Eve are by Robert Morton Nance 1873-1959. The work is considered to be in the public domain.

Chapter One

Laurel Rowan paced the weathered front porch, scanning the range road for the rooster trails of dust Chance's truck would throw up. She heaved a sigh and leaned on the thick log railing, letting the wind blow through her hair. Impatiently, she straightened up and whirled around. Snatching her large bag off the bench by the wall, she rummaged for her cell phone. Chance was never late, why would he pick today of all days to not show up on time?

Her pony tail swished behind her as she stalked over to the post at the top of the stairs and leaned a hip against it. She glanced at the cell phone screen before starting the call to check how many bars were showing.

"I'm just turning in the lane." Chance answered before the phone barely had a chance to ring.

The sun flashed off the windshield as the blue pickup came around the last bend at the top of the small coulee. Dust settled as he stopped in the yard. Laurel tossed her phone back in the bag and looped it over her shoulder before she jumped down the three shallow steps. Waving, she ran lightly across the grass toward him. Chance stepped out of the cab and removed his hat, slapping it on his thigh. The November sun slanted across the prairie, highlighting his strong features and intensifying the blue of his eyes.

"Where's Carlene? I thought she was coming with us." Laurel glanced at the empty cab.

"She changed her mind." Chance shuffled his feet and dropped his gaze.

"What do you mean…changed her mind?" She pressed him for more information.

"Dang it, Laurel. I told her I didn't want her to come."

"What? Why would you do that?"

He mumbled something she didn't catch, slapped his Stetson back on his head and climbed into the truck.

Laurel yanked open the passenger door, threw the bag onto the seat and swung up into the high cab. She fastened her seat belt and turned toward the boy behind the wheel. He'd stuck sunglasses on his face and she couldn't read his expression.

"C'mon, spill. What's up with you?"

"Ain't nothin', let it lie, will you?" Chance started the truck and slid it into gear.

"It is so something. You think I can't tell when something's bothering you? You and Carlene have a fight?" Laurel poked him in the arm with her finger.

"Leave off, I'm trying to drive."

"You tell me right now or I'm getting out right here." She made a show of reaching for the buckle of the seatbelt. Strong fingers closed over her hand, stopping her motions. Startled, Laurel looked down at the tanned hand that covered hers before meeting his gaze. The truck rolled to a stop as Chance engaged the clutch. She swallowed hard, discomforted by the intensity in his face.

"Don't be an idiot." A dark flush coloured his cheeks under the day old stubble. "Ever since you got back from England last year, you've been different somehow. I never know what you're thinking any more…" His voice trailed off and he released her hand. Dipping his head so the brim of the Stetson threw his face into shadow, Chance released the clutch and allowed the pickup to gather speed.

"Oh, okay, I guess." Laurel rolled the window down, using it as an excuse to look away from the boy she'd known all her life who was suddenly a stranger. "I thought Carlene wanted to come and meet Gramma Bella. I just know I'm going to find her today."

"If we find her, there'll be plenty of time for Carly to visit her with you. What does your dad think of all this, anyway?"

She hesitated before answering. "Dad doesn't exactly know where I'm going today. He thinks we're just going into Lethbridge for the day."

"You think that's wise, Laurie? Your dad'll be madder than a wet hen when he finds out."

"Don't call me Laurie," she protested. "You know I hate that name."

"Okay, Laurel, what are you going to tell him when he finds out? And he will," Chance continued when she opened her mouth to protest. "Mister Rowan is not a stupid man and you, missy, couldn't keep a secret if you tried."

"I don't know, but Mom is on my side…and I can so keep a secret, so there." She resisted the urge to stick her tongue out at him.

He snorted in disbelief. "Can not."

"You still didn't tell me why you came by yourself."

"Leave it alone, Laurel." Chance slowed at the end of the lane and glanced both ways before pulling out onto the paved highway.

"C 'mon, spill it." She poked him in the ribs hard enough to make him wince.

Flashing her an angry glance, he sighed and shook his head. "Fine. I told her not to come so I could spend some time with you. Alone." His jaw clenched.

"What?" Laurel struggled to process his words and the meaning behind them.

"We used to hang out together, now it's like you don't have the time of day for me anymore."

"That's just plain stupid and you know it." Heat rose in face. "We spend tons of time together, we still belong to all the same clubs. I just don't get what you're so fired up about."

"You used to be over at our place all the time. Seemed like I couldn't turn around without trippin' over you. Now I never see you unless you're with Carly."

"I guess maybe I just grew up a bit. You always acted like you were mad at me for trailing behind you. One of your friends called me your buckle bunny last spring. I'm nobody's buckle bunny."

"Yeah, I straightened Ty out about that. You never let a bit of name calling bother you before, though."

Chance quit talking and concentrated on the road, but Laurel was pretty sure he still had something stuck in his craw.

"All you ever talk about to Carly about is that guy in Cornwall.

"He's my friend!" she defended herself.

"Friends with benefits?"

"Are you freaking kidding me? That's the stupidest thing I've ever heard. Get your mind out of the gutter, Chance Cosgrove."

"The way you carry on when you get an email from him, you can't blame a guy for thinking it's more than just friends."

"Shut up, Chance. Just shut up."

Laurel scrunched down in the seat as far as the seatbelt would let her and refused to look across the cab at the driver. The vehicle slowed as they went through Lundbreck.

"Do you want to stop for anything? This is the last place before we head north into the mountains."

Laurel shook her head, still refusing to look at him. Out of the corner of her eye she saw the rise and fall of his shoulders as he shrugged. Once out of Lundbreck he picked up speed again. At the junction of Highway 3 and 22, Chance turned north on 22. The road wound its way through the towering mountains, the poplar trees were bare of the brilliant gold leaves, leaving only stark branches showing against the blue green of the conifers. Usually, Laurel loved this drive but her annoyance with Chance soured the experience. It was the last time this year she'd be able to go this way before the National Parks closed the highway at Highwood House.

Chance seemed as disinclined to talk as she was. She plugged her MP3 player into the dock and set it to play to break the awkward silence. No luck with getting a radio or cell phone signal this deep in the wilderness.

* * *

Two and a half hours later Chance pulled the pickup into the parking lot by the Shell in Bragg Creek. "Where do we go from here?"

Laurel pulled the crumpled envelope out of her pocket and smoothed it out. The return address was a bit smudged, but it was still legible. "It's on White Avenue, number one-thirty-two."

"Do you know where that is? What street are we on now?" Chance craned his neck to read the street sign. "We're at Balsam Avenue right now."

"No idea, I should have brought a map. There's the post office, let's ask there." Laurel opened the door and slid down out of the truck. "Are you coming?" She turned to look at Chance.

"Nah, I'll just wait here." He switched off the truck.

"Suit yourself." Laurel shrugged and turned her collar up against the wind whipping through the tiny parking lot. She ignored the surge of irritation. Chance had a burr under his saddle, that was for sure. What was so difficult about coming with her to the post office? And what was with his acting jealous of Coll? Reaching her destination, she pulled open the door and banished all thoughts of Coll and Chance. Today was about finding Gramma Bella.

There was no one waiting so Laurel smiled at the lady who was sorting mail behind the counter.

"How can I help you?" The woman set the bundle of letters down and came to the counter.

"I need to know where White Avenue is and how to get there from here."

"Where are you parked?"

"Over by the Shell station."

"Go out onto Balsam and turn right, at the stop sign turn right again. Then take the first right, that's White Avenue. What address are you looking for?"

"One-thirty-two. I think my gramma lives there."

"What's your grandmother's name?" The woman peered at Laurel intently.

"Bella." She shuffled her feet, unnerved by the directness of the post mistress' stare.

"Humph, Bella never mentioned having a granddaughter. Fact is, the woman never talks about her family, come to think of it."

"So, she does still live here?" A thrill of excitement spiraled through her as she waited for the response.

The woman nodded. "Her place is just outside of town. Follow White Avenue out past the old trading post and along the river. Just as you go up the hill, there's a point of ground that sticks out, the driveway is on your right before the crest of the hill. Be careful turning in, people drive way too fast on that stretch of road."

"Thanks," Laurel called. She almost raced out the door, the ratty envelope clutched in her hand.

"I got directions," she announced when she re-joined Chance.

"Where do we go from here?' He turned on the ignition and slid the shifter into first gear, the clutch still depressed.

"Go out onto Balsam, which is right there, and then turn right at the stop sign." She pointed at the busy corner.

The truck reversed and after Chance made the right turn, he glanced at Laurel. "Which way now?"

She consulted the notes she scrawled on the back of the envelope. "Take the first right, it should be White Avenue."

They stopped at the four way stop and waited their turn. "Yeah, the sign says White Avenue. So far so good." Chance made the turn after the large truck coming down highway 22 went through. "Look for street numbers, will you, Laurel?" The narrow road was hemmed in with tall spruce and fir and still looked a bit the worse for wear from the huge flood of June 2013. A number of damaged houses were up for sale.

They passed the Barbeque Steak House. "We're at fifty. There was a sign on that restaurant we just passed."

"Keep looking, I hope we're going in the right direction," Chance sounded doubtful.

"There was no other way to go, this road started at that four way stop." Laurel continued to watch for street signs.

Another restaurant was on the right. "Bavarian Inn, seventy-five White Avenue. The post office lady said to watch out for an old trading post, it must be further along."

"Look, there's the river." Chance pointed ahead where the thick growth of trees thinned out.

"There's the trading post." Laurel bounced with excitement as the pickup rounded a wide curve in the road. The land rose sharply upward on the left, the road ran beside the river on the right.

"This is where they filmed a lot of that old TV show, North of 60," Chance remarked.

"I didn't know that," Laurel said. "Okay, when we get to that bit of hill up ahead, the driveway should be on the right part way up. Lady said we can't miss it."

Half way up the hill a gate stood open at the end of a short drive. Chance pulled in and let the engine idle. "Now what? Are you sure this is the place?"

"The address is right," Laurel said.

Chance killed the engine and turned to look at her. "Do you want me to come with you or would you rather do this on your own?"

Laurel swallowed, her mouth suddenly dry. "What if she doesn't remember me? Or doesn't want to talk to me? Maybe we should just go home."

"I didn't drive almost three hours for you to turn tail and run, Laurel." Chance glared at her. "C'mon, I'll go with you"

Feeling like a hundred elephants were sitting on her chest, she got out of the truck and came around the front to join him.

"Ready?" he asked.

"Not really, but let's do it anyway." Laurel found it hard to get the words past the lump in her throat.

Three broad shallow steps led up to a small porch. Laurel raised her hand to knock, but hesitated. A hundred doubts racing through her thoughts. She half turned to run back to the truck, but then whirled back and knocked loudly on the red painted door.

Chance moved nearer until his shoulder touched hers. The contact was reassuring and helped calm her anxiety and steady the racing of her heart. They waited a moment or two, but there was no response. Laurel knocked again and stepped back a pace. After a few minutes of silence, she looked up at Chance and shrugged.

"She must be out." Laurel's voice wavered a bit.

"Maybe," Chance agreed.

Chapter Two

"Are you looking for Bella?" The woman's voice startled Laurel so badly she took a quick step backward and would have landed on her butt at the bottom of the stairs if Chance hadn't stopped her fall.

"Yes, is she home, do you know?" Chance answered for Laurel as she couldn't seem to get any words to come out of her mouth.

"Depends on who you are," she replied enigmatically.

"I'm her granddaughter, Laurel," she squeaked, having finally found her voice.

The woman walked toward them and leaned on the fence separating the two properties. A slight frown creased her forehead. "Didn't know Bella had a grandchild. She never talks about her family."

"My dad and her had a fight a long time ago. I found out where she was from a friend," Laurel explained.

"Well, you're wasting your time. Bella isn't here." The neighbor lady turned to go back to working in her garden.

"Is she going to be back soon?" Laurel persisted.

"Not for me to say. Bella doesn't like people knowing her business."

"Please." Her throat felt tight and her eyes stung with unshed tears. "I really need to talk to her. I have a message from an old friend of hers."

The woman straightened up and came back to the fence. "No need for theatrics, young woman. Tears won't get you anywhere with me. Where do you live?"

"What's that got to do with anything?" Chance demanded.

"A body can't be too careful with personal information. How do I know you're who you claim to be?"

"I live on a ranch near Pincher Creek. It belonged to my Grampa D'Arcy and he passed it on to my dad," Laurel volunteered.

"Hmmpf" the neighbor lady mumbled. She stood for a minute with her head down, twirling the end of her hoe in the dirt. "What's your momma's name?"

Chance took Laurel's arm and pulled her toward the truck. "C'mon, this isn't getting us nowhere. Let's go back to the post office and see if she moved recently and left a forwarding address."

Laurel dug in her heels and pulled free of his grip. "Anna, Mom's name is Anna. Now are you going to tell me if Gramma Bella is around or not?"

The neighbor lady heaved a huge sigh and leaned the hoe against the fence. "You might as well come over and have some tea. It's a long story."

"Really? This is still her place?" Excitement lent a high pitch to her voice. "We found her, Chance. We found her." Laurel danced in a circle around him.

"Hold your horses, Laurie. Wait and see what the woman has to say before you get all fired up," Chance cautioned.

"Don't be such a sceptic, and don't call me Laurie!"

"Are you two coming or not?" The woman stood with her hands on her hips and a stern expression on her face. "You can leave your vehicle where it is, young man. Nobody's going to bother it." She tramped toward the back door of her house.

Laurel let herself through the little gate built into the low fence between the yards. "C'mon, Chance. I don't want to go by myself."

"Fine, but I don't think we're gonna get anything worthwhile out of her." He followed Laurel through the gate and down the stone path.

"Come in, come in," she waved them toward a bright yellow table in the centre of the room, "sit wherever you like, just watch out for Gemma, that cat loves to sleep on the chairs."

Silently, Laurel sat at the table after dutifully checking the chair for sleeping cats. Chance sat opposite her and raised an eyebrow in amusement.

"I'm Ally, I promised Bella I'd look after her place for her. Why are you two looking for her again?"

"When I was in Cornwall, when my mom was so sick, I stayed with an old friend of my gramma's. I found some old letters from Gramma Bella to Sarie. She's the lady I stayed with. She told me Gramma is still alive," Laurel explained.

"Why would you think she was dead?" Ally appeared astounded.

"Because my parents led me to believe she was. They never actually said it, they just implied it and never clarified if what I thought was true was really the truth."

"Must have been some argument your father had with her." Ally leaned closer, a gleam in her eye at the thought of juicy gossip.

"It was over my grandfather," Laurel said bluntly, but offered no more explanation.

"He's dead though, isn't he?" Ally prodded.

"Grampa D'Arcy is gone, yes," Laurel agreed. There was no way in hell she was going to mention Vear Du to the woman.

"Where is Laurel's gramma, then?" Chance broke into the conversation. "You said you're looking after the place while she's gone. Where is she?"

Laurel sent him a smile of thanks for steering the conversation back on track.

"Well, now that's a story, isn't it?" Ally poured tea into the three mugs before setting the pot on the table. "Your grandmother is quite an interesting woman with a very eccentric outlook on life."

"You sound like you don't like her all that much," Laurel declared. Chance put a hand on her arm to remind Laurel to keep her temper in check.

"Quite the opposite, my dear, quite the opposite. Bella and I get along famously. We're like two peas in a pod." Ally laughed and sipped her tea, blue eyes smiling at her over the rim.

"So, tell us the story," Chance demanded.

"Drink your tea, son. I'll tell you what I know in good time."

Laurel dutifully lifted the mug to her lips. Chance took a swallow of his and promptly spit it out.

"What is that stuff?" He wiped at his shirt front. "It tastes like swamp water."

Laurel giggled and handed him the towel Ally threw on the table.

"Devil's Claw tea, it's good for you," Ally told him.

"I'll stick to water, thanks." Chance shoved the mug as far away from him as he could.

Laurel took another sip. It wasn't as bad as Chance made out, but it was different than anything she'd had before.

Ally settled down in a chair at the head of the table and looked from one of them to the other. "Where to begin, where to begin…" she mused.

"Try the beginning," Chance prompted.

Chapter Three

"Bella came here not long after I did," Ally began. "At first she kept to herself, but after a while we became friends. She never talked about her family much, or why she decided to move here when she could have stayed on the ranch. Over time she confided in me a bit, but only little things. She loved your mother, Laurel, and she doted on your father. I could tell just by the way she talked about them. It wasn't often she mentioned them, though. I only know your mother's name, and that Bella's father arranged a marriage with a rancher near Pincher Creek. He packed her onto the ship and washed his hands of her. I think she missed her home in Cornwall and being near the sea. I'd see her lots of times sitting down on the banks of the river listening to the water rush by."

"Can you get to the point and tell us where she is?" Chance interrupted the torrent of words.

"Yes, please, can you tell us where she is?" Laurel pleaded.

Ally paused and stared hard at Laurel, who repressed the urge to squirm under the scrutiny. Apparently having made up her mind about something, Ally took a deep breath and let it out slowly, the air hissing softly between her teeth.

"Bella came flying over here all in a tizzy, asking if I would keep an eye on her place while she was gone. She was right upset, almost in tears, and frantic to get on the road as fast as possible. Of course I told her I'd watch the place. It's no trouble at all, really. Anyway, she lit out of here like a cat with its tail on fire. I haven't heard from her since."

"Where did she go?" Laurel ground her teeth in frustration.

Ally looked at her queerly. "Why to the airport, of course, dear."

"She flew somewhere?" Laurel clenched her hands into fists in her lap.

"Yes, young lady, she did. How else could she get to England in a hurry?" Ally waved her hand across the table toward Laurel and Chance. "Come now, drink up your tea and I'll tell you what I know."

Laurel groaned inwardly. Getting information out of Ally was like pulling hen's teeth. Dutifully, she took a sip of the tea. Chance eyed the concoction and pushed his cup further away from him.

"Not thirsty, sorry, m'am," he apologized.

Ally settled back in her chair and stroked the huge orange cat that sprang into her lap.

"As I was saying, Bella came charging over here all upset. I couldn't understand what she was going on about until she calmed down some. An old friend of hers called with some bad news. Somebody Bella cared about was sick or hurt. Maybe she said they were missing? I don't rightly recall the details, though the up-shoot of it is, Bella went running off to England."

"Did she say who called? Was it Coll?" Laurel leaned forward in her chair. "Did she mention who was in trouble?"

Chance snorted and frowned at the mention of Coll's name and Laurel laid a hand on his knee under the table warning him not to interrupt now that the woman seemed to be on a roll.

Ally scratched the big tom under the chin and her forehead crinkled as she frowned. "It was a funny name she told me, a friend from when she was young—"

"Sarie, was it Sarie who called?" Laurel broke in.

"It's not polite to interrupt someone when they're speaking," Ally reprimanded her. "They sure don't teach manners in school anymore, do they" She caught Laurel's gaze and raised an eyebrow.

"I'm sorry for being rude," she apologized to the older woman. "But was it Sarie who called?"

"Thank you, dear. Apology accepted." She took a sip of tea. "Yes, I do believe that's the name she kept repeating. Sarie, is it. Short for Sarah, I presume."

"I'm not sure what her real name is, she just goes by Sarie."

Do you know where in England she was headed?" Chance turned the conversation back to the matter at hand.

"Her old home, where she grew up. Some odd name…Penwith, Pendeen…it started with pen, at any rate."

"Penzance? Is that it? I'm pretty sure she grew up in Penzance, 'cause Sarie lives near there and Emily, another one of her friends, still lives there."

"Yes, dear, I think you're right. It was Penzance."

"Who is missing or hurt? Did she tell you anything about that?" Laurel twirled her mug of tea between her palms, watching the pale green liquid swirl like a tiny whirl pool.

Ally reached across the table and put a hand on her arm. "Stop that, girl. You're going to spill on my nice clean tablecloth."

Chance pushed his chair back and stood up. "We gotta go soon or we'll never get home in time for chores."

"Don't be in such a hurry, young man. I don't get many visitors and I'm enjoying your unexpected company. But if you're in such a hurry…it was another odd name. I thought she was saying 'oh dear, oh dear' but apparently she was saying—"

Vear! She was saying Vear Du, wasn't she?" Laurel stood up in her excitement.

"Why, yes, that's exactly what she kept repeating. Such an odd name. Is it male or female?"

"It's the man she was in love with as a teenager, before she came to Canada."

"When did she leave?"

Laurel smiled at Chance. She could always trust him to get to the point. Caught up in trying to pry information out of the woman, she'd totally forgotten to find out how long Gramma Bella had been gone.

"Let me see if I can remember exactly when she left." Ally paused and looked over Laurel's head for a minute or two. "Yes, it was right near Hallowe'en, so about two weeks ago. Bella called it some weird name, though instead of Hallowe'en."

"Guy Fawkes Day," Chance suggested.

"No, it wasn't that. It sounded like Sowen, but she said it had nothing to do with pigs. Your grandmother was more than a bit odd sometimes."

"She meant Samhain, it's spelled nothing like it sounds, but that's what she was talking about. It's one of the cross quarter days and it used to mark the beginning of a new year in the old Celtic calendar. It's a time of year when the veil between the worlds is thin and those who have passed on can come back and visit. In Mexico they call it the Feast of the Dead and leave offerings on the graves of their loved ones.

"If you say so, dear. That's all a little beyond me, I'm afraid," Ally replied.

"We really gotta get going, Laurel." Chance edged toward the door.

"I'm coming, just give me a sec."

She waited until the door swung shut behind him before she spoke.

"Thanks for letting me know where Gramma Bella is, Ally. And thanks for looking after her place while she's gone. Now I know where she is, I'm gonna come and visit as often as I can. Even if Dad doesn't approve."

"In that case I look forward to seeing more of you, Laurel. Now you better scat or your boyfriend's gonna leave without you." Ally patted her arm.

"He's not my boyfriend," she protested.

Ally laughed. "A body would have to be blind not to see the way he looks at you. Take it from an old lady, that boy has feelings for you."

“Thanks again, I really do have to get going, but I wanted to let you know how much I appreciate the information.”

“Run along, dear.”

“Bye, and thanks again.” Laurel opened the door and ran down the shallow steps. Chance had already turned the truck around with its nose pointed at the gate. She got in and hardly had the door shut before the pickup was rolling forward.

Chapter Four

"What do you think, Chance? She's kind of an odd duck. I wonder if I should call Sarie, or Coll. They should know if Gramma Bella is back in Penzance." Laurel tucked a foot underneath her and half-turned toward Chance.

"Sure, go ahead and call Coll, if that's what you want." His lip curled and a frown darkened his face. "Why not call the girl you met over there, Ashleen, or something?"

"I could, I guess. I might call her anyway. What's wrong with me calling Coll?"

"Nothing, I guess," he muttered. "If your gramma really is in Cornwall, what are you gonna do?"

"I don't know, this is getting more complicated by the minute. I was counting on her being home when we got there. I can't tell Dad, he'll go postal when he finds out I've even been looking for Gramma."

“"Can you talk to your mom, then? Will she understand better?" Chance took his eyes off the road long enough to glance over at her.

"Yeah, I'm gonna tell Mom as soon as I get home. She'll know what to do."

"You wanna stop and grab a sub or something in town before we head out?"

Laurel nodded and Chance pulled into the small plaza by the gas station. After a quick meal, they headed toward Pincher Creek. Chance seemed disinclined to talk, so Laurel was left alone with her thoughts.

It was dark by the time Chance dropped her off. She waved good-bye before taking the steps in one leap. The lights were on in the kitchen and her dad's office. Laurel pussy-footed down the hall past the open door of the office. In the kitchen, Mom was chopping vegetables at the counter.

"Hey, Mom." She grabbed a can of pop from the fridge and sat down at the table. "Can I help with anything?"

"Nope, I have everything under control. Did you find what you were looking for in Lethbridge? You were gone longer than usual. You and Carly lose track of time?" Anna Rowan pushed a lock of hair off her forehead with the back of her hand.

"No, actually, we didn't go to Lethbridge."

"Was there something in Medicine Hat you wanted?"

Laurel shook her head. "We didn't go to the Hat, either. It was really weird, though. Carly didn't come, it was just Chance and me."

'Is Carly sick or something?" Mom caught her gaze across the kitchen island.

"No, Chance asked her not to come. He said he wanted it to be just him and me. And he got all prickly every time I mentioned Coll's name. What's up with that?"

Anna laid the paring knife down and came to sit at the table beside Laurel. "Why do you think he'd do that?"

"Beats me, we've been friends forever, and the three of us always do things together."

"I think Chance is interested in you, sweetie. Has he asked you to go out with him?"

"No! I mean, I like him and all, but not that way. It'd be like kissing my brother or something." Laurel made a face and grimaced.

"Just keep it in mind, that maybe the boy sees you as more than a friend now that you've all grown up a bit."

Laurel nodded and snagged a banana from the bowl on the table.

"So, if you didn't go to Lethbridge or the Hat, where did the pair of you go?"

"Chance drove me up to Bragg Creek." She watched her mom's face carefully for her reaction.

"What did you find in Bragg Creek? What made you want to go there?" Anna frowned and got up to move back to the counter, avoiding looking directly as her daughter.

"I went looking for Gramma Bella, I know she's not dead," she blurted out.

"Your father and I never told you she was dead, where did ever get that idea?"

"Mom, look at me. You both let me believe she was dead, not just moved away. When I was visiting Sarie, I found a bunch of letters from Gramma Bella to her. The return address on the latest one was Bragg Creek."

"I wish you'd mentioned this before and not gone haring off to find her on your own."

"I didn't think Dad would let me go if he knew where I was going. Mom, what did they fight about that upset things so badly that she moved out and nobody ever mentioned her again?"

"I'm afraid that's something you need to ask your father about. Now tell me, did you get a chance to speak to Bella?"

"She wasn't home. The neighbor lady said she went off to Cornwall in a big hurry about two weeks ago."

"Cornwall? You're sure the woman said she went to Cornwall, not London?"

Laurel nodded. "Ally, the next door neighbor, said Gramma Bella got a call from Sarie that someone was in trouble, and then she left in a big hurry."

"Hmmm, I wonder…Bella vowed she'd never set foot back in Penzance. She believed the ruckus and embarrassment she endured when she left would never be forgotten. She never wanted to run into Daniel Treliving ever again."

"Daniel Treliving? That's Gort's uncle. I don't blame her, he was a real jack ass."

"I didn't realize you knew him, what was he like? Is he really as nasty as Bella made out/" Anna stopped stirring a pot on the stove and leaned a hip on the counter.

"I never really met him, but I did see him sometimes. He was Gort's guardian, but he treated him like crap. Used him for a punching bag, so Gort would hideout at Sarie's or Emily's. But Gramma Bella doesn't have to worry about seeing him, he's dead now."

"Are you sure? When did you find this out?"

"Coll emailed me about it, and so did Ash, and Gort too when he was feeling better. He's living with Emily and Coll now."

"That's very interesting. I wonder who is in such trouble that Bella would throw caution to the wind and take off for England.

"Ally said it was Vear Du who was in trouble."

Anna's face went white and gripped the counter hard enough to turn her knuckles white. "Are you sure?" Her voice was barely above a whisper.

"As sure as I can be." Laurel swallowed hard. "I know who he is, Mom. I know Vear Du is my grandfather. Is that what Dad and Gramma fought about? Is that why she moved away and I never saw her again."

Anna nodded and wiped a tear from her cheek. "Since you've discovered that much, I'll answer your questions as best as I can. But you should still talk with your dad about this. Your father was devastated when he found out the truth. All his life he believed D'Arcy was his dad, and in a way he was, in all the most important ways. It came as a real shock when he learned he was the son of some weird magical being."

"Was he mad at Gramma for not telling him sooner? When did he figure it out?" Laurel tried to put herself in his place and couldn't.

"He found out when you were pretty young, I thought he was going to bring the house down he was so angry."

"Is that when you found out?"

Anna shook her head. "Bella told me before I married your father. She thought it wasn't fair to let me marry him without know exactly what I was getting into. It took your dad a while to get over that too. Me knowing, and not telling him."

"Mom, Aisling invited me to spend Christmas with her family, are you okay with that? I've been saving my money to pay for the plane fare since I got home last time. I didn't know Ash was going to ask me to come for Christmas, though. Can I go? I really want to find Gramma Bella, too. If Vear Du is in trouble maybe Ash and I can help him somehow."

"Let me talk to your father about all this and I'll let you know what he says. Leave it with me for a bit, okay?"

Chapter Five

"Dad!" Laurel stamped her foot. "Why can't I go?"

"Don't you stamp your foot at me, young lady," Colt Rowan spoke evenly.

"You're being so unfair. I have the money to pay for plane fare." Laurel tried to lower her voice.

"It's not about being fair, Laurel."

"Then what is it about?" she demanded.

"Watch your tone of voice," her dad warned.

"Fine." She twirled a piece of hair around her finger and clenched her teeth.

"Laurel, honey. Try to see your dad's point of view." Anna Rowan tried to make peace with her warring family.

"I don't understand his point of view. What's so wrong about wanting to go and visit Ash, and Gort, and Coll?"

"I don't like you hanging around boys I've never met. Why can't you give Chance a break?" Colton argued.

"What's Chance got to do with me going to Cornwall?" Laurel rounded on her dad.

"Nothing, other than he's good kid and he worships the ground you walk on."

"Dad! He's like my brother. You're imagining things." She let herself be distracted for a moment.

"Colt, don't push the boy on her," Anna warned her husband.

"There's nothing wrong with the boy. His parent's land abuts ours, it's going to be his one day. It only seems natural that the two of them should get together," he continued.

"Hey, I'm still here. Quit talking like I'm not in the room," Laurel broke in.

"You're right, sweetie. Sorry," her mom said.

"Aisling asked me to stay with her, at her house. It's not like I'm going to be staying at Emily's in the same house as Coll," she argued.

"I don't like it," Colton growled.

"It's Christmas, Laurel. Don't you want to be home for Christmas?" Her dad tried a different tack.

"What if I went now and came home just before Christmas? I could fly on Christmas Eve, or the twenty-third," she suggested.

"That might work, Colton," Anna said. "There's no harm in her wanting to see her friends."

"Who's going to make sure she doesn't get into trouble? We don't even know this girl's parents. That Sarah, or Sarie, or whatever her name is, I don't trust her one bit. She was in cahoots with my mother all that time ago," Colton warmed to his subject.

"You could call and talk to Ash's parents," Laurel attempted to sidetrack her father before he really got wound up.

"We could call them," Anna said.

"Whose side are you on? Are you saying you think her going is a good idea?" Colton demanded.

"I remember what it was like being her age and liking a boy my parent's didn't approve of." She lifted an eyebrow and smiled gently. Her husband had the grace to blush.

"That was different," he muttered.

"How is it different?" Laurel demanded. "If you like Chance so much, you hook up with him!" She turned on her heel and stormed out of the room. She let the porch door slam behind her and jumped down the step. She slapped the hat she'd grabbed on the way on onto her head and crossed the yard to the barn. Even though it was November, the day was fairly warm.

She stopped at the corral fence and leaned on the top rail. Laurel whistled shrilly and waited for the small herd grazing in the pasture to come to her call. Sam threw his head up and whinnied. Wheeling on his haunches, he cantered through the open corral gate toward the fence where she stood. The buckskin gelding came to a snorting halt in front of her. Laurel reached for the halter lead shank draped over the rail and climbed over the corral fence. She fished a treat out of her jacket pocket and slipped the halter over his head. Tossing the shank over the gelding's neck, she tied the free end to the nose band of the halter.

Grasping at handful of mane, she vaulted lightly to his back. Touching him with her heel, she turned him from the fence and trotted down to the gate. Kneeing him closer, she asked Sam to side-pass against the barrier. Leaning over, she unhooked the gate and pushed it open. Keeping her hand on it she rode through, pivoting as his rump cleared the opening. Sam side-passed neatly to help her close it. Laurel pointed the horse's nose across the rolling prairie toward the Old Man River.

A herd of cattle grazed in the distance, she gave them wide berth, and they in turn ignored the horse and rider. The sun was warm though the wind had a bite to it. Laurel pulled the hat lower on her head and raised the collar of her jacket up around her ears. She was glad of the warmth of the gelding beneath her. She squinted at the position of the sun. It was low on the horizon and she reckoned she had an hour of sunlight left. Plenty of time to ride to the river bluffs and back. The gelding was content to amble along, picking his own way across the short grass prairie. She skirted the arrangement of large rocks laid out in a rough circle. The place had an oddly peaceful feeling to it. Often in the summer she'd ride out and leave Sam to graze while she walked among the stones, wondering how long they'd been there and what they represented.

Mom said people of the Blackfoot Nation created the circle a long time ago. She didn't know how long exactly or what it had been used for, but she taught Laurel to always treat it with respect and never move any of the rocks. As she passed it, Laurel dropped a bit of cornbread she kept in her pocket for Sam. It always felt right to leave some sort of offering when she came there. A little further on was a figure of a man and a giant turtle laid out on the prairie in rocks covered with rusty coloured lichen. Laurel smiled and halted Sam so she could savour the sight. It always amused her and she wondered if the figure of the man was leading the turtle, or if the turtle was chasing the man. She always thought of the stone figure as the native trickster Na'pe, Old Man, in English. That's who the Old Man River was named after, she imagined.

Shaking her head, she nudged Sam forward. She set him into a rocking lope and laughed as the wind whipped across the plains from the west. Before long she reached the clay coloured bluff overlooking the winding river far below. There were other places where trails led down into the river valley, but there was no time for that today. She let Sam drop his head and pull at the tough gamma grass. She braced her hands on his withers and watched the shadows change as the sun dropped lower. The wind whipped the grass so it rippled like the waves on the sea. Her thoughts turned back to Gramma Bella and Cornwall. *Why can't Dad see I need to follow Gramma Bella to England? And what's with Dad going on about Chance and me like he expects us to get married some day? As if!*

She pulled Sam's head up, and after taking one last look at the river valley bathed in the orange light of the setting sun, Laurel headed back toward the ranch house. Sam broke into a jog and Laurel allowed him to set the pace, sitting easily to his smooth gait. The dry grasses rustled and tumbleweeds ran before the wind, piling up against the cross fence where it joined the north pasture. She took a different route back, pausing to open and close the ranch gate set in the bob wire fence. A streamer of smoke blew almost horizontal from the chimney of the ranch house. Laurel thought of the story Harry Good Smoke told her about how the Black Foot people got their name. Periodically, the tribe would burn off sections of the prairie, controlling the burn by beating back the flames when they reached the limit of where they intended to stop. The bottoms of their moccasins became stained with soot from the ashes, and the soldiers and missionaries identified them by that mark. Of course, he explained, Black Foot was only what the white folk called them. He was proud of his heritage and still lived on the Blood Reserve. They earned the name Blood Indians from the red ochre they used to paint their faces for ceremony and ritual. He was from the Akainawa Nation, he said. The others were Siksika, and Piikuni. They used to range as far north as Ponoka, which he told her mean Elk in his language.

"P'NO'ka," she said aloud putting the emphasis on the second syllable like he'd taught her. She slapped Sam's neck and laughed. "You are an elk-dog, did you know that? When the Black Foot first saw horses they thought they were a mixture of elk and the dogs they used as beasts of burden. "P'no'ka-Imitaa." Sam shook his head and broke into a lope when she touched him with her heel.

The sky darkened as the sun slipped below the hills to the west. Her thoughts returned to figuring out a way to convince her dad to let her go visit Aisling. And Coll, she added. When she reached the corral she slid down from Sam's back and slipped the halter and shank over his head. She spent a minute rubbing his cheeks and scratching behind his ears. Sam leaned gently into her ministrations and lipped the fingers of her other hand. She pulled a crumbled krunchie from the pocket of her jeans and offered it to him. He took it and left to join the other horses when she pushed him away.

Laurel hung the halter and shank on the top rail and crawled through the fence. Dusting the hair off her butt and inner thighs, she headed toward the house. The light had mostly leaked from the sky and the sight of the yellow light streamed across the yard from the windows made her warm inside. Mom and Dad were still in the study, their figures clearly visible to her. They seemed to still be talking. She hoped Mom had convinced him to see things her way.

She knocked the dirt from her boots before climbing the steps. Laurel stooped to pet Charlie's head as she passed. The big shepherd cross mutt licked her hand and laid his head back on his paws. The warmth of the house was welcome when she stepped through the door. Once the sun went down the temperature dropped pretty quick. She shed her jacket and hung it on the rack by the wall. Standing up, she used the boot jack to pull off her boots, steadying herself with the back of the hall bench.

"Laurel, is that you?" Mom called from the kitchen.

"Yeah, I just came in." Laurel padded down the hall, wondering when Mom left the study and went to the kitchen. "Do you want help with supper?" She pushed the swinging door to the kitchen open.

"You can peel the potatoes." Mom pushed the bowl of vegetables toward her.

Laurel got a paring knife out of the drawer and settled on a stool, pulling the bowl closer. A pan of salted water sat at her elbow and as she finished peeling and cutting up the potatoes she dropped the pieces into the water. She glanced at Mom out of the corner of her eye, wondering if she dared ask if Dad had changed his mind. Her mother was humming under her breath as she rolled out dough for cinnamon buns. Sighing, she stood to put the full pot on the stove before turning back to centre island to start on the carrots.

"What's the real reason you want to go to Cornwall so badly?" Mom didn't look up, but kept plying the rolling pin.

Startled, Laurel had to think a moment before she answered. "You know I went to see Gramma Bella in Bragg Creek, but she wasn't home. If I go to Penzance to see Aisling I can see Gramma Bella, too. I'm sure she's staying with Sarie. I'm gonna email Ash tonight and find out for sure."

"How serious are you about this boy, Coll?" Mom glanced at her.

The heat rose in her face. "Umm, I don't know. What do you mean by serious? I like him fine, but we're not talking about getting married or anything. What was Dad on about with Chance? Does he think we're gonna get married? Where would he get an idea like that?" Laurel dropped a chopped carrot in the pan with more force than was necessary.

"No man wants to see his little girl grow up and become a woman. You'll always be his little baby girl," Mom tried to explain.

"What's that got to do with Chance, or Coll, for that matter?" Laurel interrupted her.

"He knows Chance, knows his family. You're our only child, sweetie. One day the ranch will be yours, if you want it. You're gonna need a good man to help you run it. Dad thinks Chance would be a good choice." Anna smiled at her, her hands busy sprinkling brown sugar, raisins and butter over the dough.

"What if I don't want to marry Chance? Don't I get some say in this?" She stood up, her temper rising.

"Of course you do, sweetie. You're too young to be worrying about getting married anyway. It's just your dad wanting to take care of you and trying to do it the best way he knows how. So, if you don't feel that way about Chance, tell me a bit more about this Coll character."

Laurel ducked her head. "There isn't much to tell…he's just different from the other guys I know. Sometimes, he makes me mad, 'cause he just doesn't get what I'm trying to say, but it never lasts and pretty soon he's doing or saying something stupid to make me laugh."

"Has he kissed you?"

"Mom! As if." Laurel let her hair fall forward to hide her red face.

"Just asking." She could tell from Mom's voice she was trying not to laugh.

"Chance tried to, kiss me, I mean," Laurel confessed.

"What did you do?" Anna stopped cutting, the knife resting on the rolled up dough and filling.

"I kinda avoided it. I just don't feel like that about him." Laurel peeked at her mother through the hair falling over her eyes.

"Was he good about it? He didn't push the issue, did he?" A small frown creased her forehead.

"He was sorta mad. Wanted to know what was wrong with me," Laurel muttered.

"I hope you told him there was nothing wrong with you." Anna laid her knife down.

"I said it was gross, like kissing my brother." She looked up and grinned. "He didn't much like that. Stormed off and didn't talk to me for the rest of the night."

"When was this?" Anna went back to cutting the cinnamon buns.

"After the last rodeo. I got a ride home with Arlen Beckett."

"It was good of Arlen to bring you home, it's a bit out of his way," Anna remarked.

"Said he didn't mind, and I offered to give him some gas money," Laurel said.

"I'm glad you remembered your manners. It was good of him, I'll have to remember to thank him next time I see him."

"Has Dad been encouraging Chance, like talking to him about his crazy idea of joining the ranches together? That's all I need. Carly's my best friend, and I can't very well avoid her brother when I'm over there all the time." Laurel put the carrots on the stove.

"I'll speak with your dad about it. If you really don't want to get involved with Chance, he's just gonna have to accept that."

"Did he change his mind about me going to Aisling's?" Laurel held her breath and crossed her fingers.

"Not yet. Laurel, I think you need to come clean and tell him about going out to find Bella. You know how he hates having things hidden from him. Maybe if you explain it to him, he'll come around. No promises, though. Whatever he decides, you're going to have to live with it," she warned.

"I'm sixteen. I can make my own decisions." Laurel stuck her chin out.

"While you live under our roof you have to abide by our rules," Anna warned her daughter. "I wouldn't go and talk to your dad with that attitude."

"I'm gonna go get changed," Laurel said.

"Dinner will be ready in twenty minutes, make sure you're down in time to set the table." Anna ruffled Laurel's hair as she passed.

She took the stairs two at a time and slid down the hall in her socks. She giggled and grabbed the door jamb of her room to stop her skid. After shedding her clothes, she showered and changed. Gathering her dirty things into a ball, she went back downstairs and tossed them into the basket in the laundry room off the mud room. Laurel hesitated as she passed the study door. It stood ajar and she could hear her dad talking to someone on the phone.

Better not disturb him, she thought. It was going to be a hard enough sell as it was. She made short work of setting the table, poking her head into the kitchen to ask if Harry was joining them for dinner.

"Harry's headed into town so he'll get something to eat there," Anna answered.

Laurel removed the extra place setting and turned the light on over the table. In answer to her mom's call she pushed through the door into the kitchen and took the platter of meat from her. She went back for the vegetable bowls, inhaling the intoxicating scent of the baking cinnamon buns. Mom made the best sticky buns Laurel had ever tasted.

Dad came out of the study right on schedule as Mom carried the last bowl out to the table. She smiled at him and he dropped a quick kiss on her head. Laurel rolled her eyes. There was something embarrassing about seeing her parents being mushy. It made her very uncomfortable to think about her parents being interested in each other that way.

After Laurel finished helping with the supper dishes she went upstairs to do her homework. Closing the math book with a relieved sigh, she went in search of a snack. Wandering down the stairs, she looked into the living room where Mom was stitching at her needlework and watching a sit com. She hesitated outside the study and then chickened out and continued on to the kitchen. Scrounging into the fridge for something to snack on, she pulled out a brick of cheddar cheese and a green apple. She added some crackers to the sliced fruit and cheese and returned the items to the fridge. Pulling up a stool, she sat at the island and satisfied her hunger. She washed and dried the things she used and wandered back out into the hall.

Laurel listened at the door to the study, it didn't sound like Dad was talking to anyone so he was probably working on the books. Fall branding hadn't been over for too long, and she knew he'd sent some yearling steers and some replacement heifers to Balog's auction mart in Lethbridge. She knocked on the door and pushed it open.

"Hey, Laurel. What do you want?" Dad laid down the pen and rubbed his eyes. Leaning back in the chair he scrubbed his hands through his hair, the rich blue black strands peppered with silver.

"If you're busy, I can come back later." Laurel started to chicken out.

"No, I could use a break. What do you want to talk about?"

"I wish you wouldn't encourage Chance. I don't like him that way. He's like my brother, or something," she began.

Colton Rowan held up his hand to stop the flow of words. "Your mother has already read me the riot act, chapter and verse, on that subject. I apologize if it seemed as if I was pushing you into something you don't want any part of."

"Okay, thanks." Laurel twirled a strand of hair around her fingers. The silence stretched between them but she couldn't make herself bring up the subject she really wanted to talk about.

"Was there something else, pet? I really should finish the books." He picked up the pen.

"Daddy, I really want to go and see Ash. Can I, please? I promise I'll behave and I'll come home before Christmas if you want," she blurted out the words before she could change her mind.

Colt put the pen back down and tented his fingers, resting his chin on the forefingers. She forced herself not to squirm under his intense regard. Although she wanted badly to continue to plead her case, Laurel stayed quiet. Mom always said if she would just be patient and let Dad come to his own conclusions without pestering him, more things would turn out in her favour.

"You really want to do this, princess? I'm not crazy about the idea of you not being home for the holidays."

"I really do want to go. And…" she hesitated on the verge of telling him about Gramma Bella, "please don't be mad. I went to Bragg Creek to find Gramma." She waited for him to lose his cool.

"Did you see her?" he spoke calmly. The cords in his neck grew taut as he clenched his teeth.

"No, her neighbor said she went to England 'cause Sarie called and said Vear Du was in trouble." Laurel waited for the explosion she was sure was coming.

"In trouble, is he? What should that have to do with my mother after all this time?"

"I think she must still care about him," Laurel ventured a reply. "So, if I go to see Aisling I can see Gramma Bella too without it bothering you."

"Laurel, whether you see her there or here, it will still bother me. The woman lied to me for most of my life and now you and your mother expect me to just forgive her and welcome her back into the fold." Colton pressed his lips together into a thin line. "I just can't do it."

"I know you're mad at her, but she's my gramma and I want to see her again. I'm not mad at her," Laurel argued, knowing she was pushing her luck.

Dad sighed and rubbed his eyes again, leaning back in the chair and gazing at the ceiling. "Your mother made the same argument earlier. You're a smart girl, and I guess you are old enough to know what's right and what's wrong. If you really and truly want to go half way across the world to see your friends and track down your grandmother, I shouldn't stand in your way."

"Daddy, thank you!" Laurel leaped to her feet and flung her arms around his neck. "I'll be good, I promise. Thank you, thank you." She hugged him hard and felt the vibration of his chest when he laughed.

"I can't win when both the women in my life gang up against me. But, just don't expect me to welcome the woman into my home. Do I make myself clear?"

"Yes, Dad. Perfectly. I won't ask her home for dinner."

"How did you get to Bragg Creek anyway?" A frown darkened his face.

"I talked Chance into taking me. Carly was supposed to come too, but he told her not to come."

Colton laughed. "You've got that boy wrapped around your little finger."

"I didn't ask him to get all weird and mushy. I like things the way they were before he got all crazy," she protested.

"What do you mean? Did that idiot try something with you?" Dad half rose to his feet.

"No, not really. He's just so…so, serious," she said hastily.

"You let me know if the young pup steps out of line, you hear me?"

"Yes, Daddy," she said meekly. Inside she was shouting for joy. Laurel could hardly believe her dad was going to let her fly to England.

"Off you go, princess. I have a lot of paperwork to get through yet. Go tell your mom the news. I know you two will have a lot of planning to do." He kissed her forehead and unwrapped her arms from his neck.

"Thanks, Dad." She kissed his cheek and danced out of the study.

"Mom," she hollered after she closed the door behind her. "Dad says I can go!" She ran down the hall and jumped on the couch beside her mom. Anna set her needlework down and hugged Laurel.

"I'm happy for you. Just make sure you stay safe." Anna held her at arm's length and studied her face.

"I will, I promise. Can I call Ash right now? Oh, what time is it there?"

“It might be better if you email her and figure out a time to call when it works for both of you,” Anna suggested.

“Thanks, Mom.” Laurel bounded out of the room and took the stairs two at a time, skidding down the hall and into her room.

Chapter Six

Carly hugged Laurel so tight her ribs hurt. "I wish you could come with me, Carly." Laurel extracted herself from her best friend's grip.

"Me, too. But Dad wouldn't hear of it. Missing a week of school, not to mention the expense. Make sure you email me every day, and post tons of pictures on line. It'll almost be like I'm there with you." Carly gave her quick hug and stepped back. "You need to go through security soon, so go say good bye to your folks."

"Still, I'd love for you to meet Aisling, Gort, and Coll." She glanced around the crowded baggage check in area. "Where's Chance? I thought he might show up to say good bye."

A red flush rose up Carly's face. "He didn't want to. Why is he mad at you? Did you two have a fight or something?"

Laurel shook her head. "I don't know, he's been strange ever since I came home. And he gets all snarly whenever Coll's name comes up. What's with that?"

"Are you blind? It's plain as day how he feels about you." Carly sighed in exasperation.

"How he feels about me? What's to see? He's one of my oldest friends."

"Chance has the hots for you and you never seem to give him a second look," Carly explained.

"What?" Laurel was astounded at her friend's revelation. "Really? You've got to be kidding me."

"God's honest truth." Carly laid a hand over her heart.

"Seriously? Man, I gotta go, but we're gonna talk more about this later. It just feels so unreal." Laurel picked up her carry-on luggage and gave her mom a hug. Dad was as bad as Chance, refusing to come to airport to see her off. Once Gramma Bella was back home, she'd have to find a way to get the two of them together and resolve whatever the problems there were between them.

Laurel paused by the entrance to security and looked back at Carly and Mom one more time. Mom had her arm around Carly's shoulders and they both waved. She got through the line up in record time and set out to find her gate. Once there, she pulled out her tablet to finish the last chapters of a book she needed to read for school.

After a long and boring trip across the ocean in the plane, Laurel was more than happy to collect her luggage and catch the Heathrow Express from the airport to Paddington Station. She had a ticket for the Cornish Riviera Express where Mom had booked her a berth with a bed and wash basin all to herself. The hustle and bustle of Paddington Station unnerved Laurel when she first stepped off the Heathrow train. *Damn, I wish Carly was here.* Rolling the large suitcase along beside her, Laurel stopped at the ticket office to ask where she should wait to board the night train. The attendant showed her to a well-appointed lounge and told her someone would come and let her know when the train was available to board.

Her feet resting on her suitcase, Laurel flipped through a magazine someone left on the chair beside her. She tossed it back where it came from and closed her eyes. Excitement warred with weariness. It was so hard to believe she was back in England. It didn't seem real at all. In just a few hours she'd be stepping off the train in Penzance. Hopefully, it would be a clear day and Saint Michael's Mount would be visible off to the east across Mount's Bay. *I wonder if I'll see Corm again, if we go there. Only this time I'll know he's the spirit of Cormoran, the last giant ever seen in Cornwall. The first time I thought he was just a nice old man.* Her thoughts drifted to what Carly said about her brother. How had she missed the fact Chance wanted to be more than friends? He had tons of girls chasing after him at school and at high school rodeo events.

"The Cornish Riviera Express is now available for boarding. Please have your boarding passes ready," a First Great Western Rail employee announced.

Startled out of her thoughts, Laurel got to her feet and collected her things. She exited the lounge. Even at this hour of the evening Paddington was busy. Pushing her way through the milling crowds she searched the overhead information boards to find the track for her train. She finally found it and started off toward Platform One. She stopped beside the long sleek blue car emblazoned with *Night Riviera Sleeper.* A man in a First Great Western uniform approached and Laurel showed him her ticket.

"I'm sorry, but I don't know how to find my berth. Can you help me, please?" Laurel was totally at a loss to figure out which car to get on, and how she was supposed to figure out which berth was hers.

The man explained how to read the ticket and took her to the correct car. "Once you're on board, the berth numbers are on the doors. If you have any trouble, there should be an attendant around to help you out."

"Thank you so much," Laurel said and allowed the man to lift her luggage on board.

"You'll be all right then, miss?" he asked.

"Yes, thank you again," she replied, although she was still a bit nervous. The last time she rode the train, it was daylight and she had a seat in the first class car. Finding her place then was so much easier than in this narrow corridor with windows on one side and a bank of closed doors on the other stretching the length of the car.

Another uniformed gentleman came to her rescue and showed her to the correct door and explained how things worked. Laurel thanked him and stowed her belongings. She swayed a little as the train pulled out of the station. Once it was well underway, Laurel went off in search of the Lounge Car for something to eat. Happily, it was easy to find and Laurel was soon back in her berth and ready for bed. Snuggled under the duvet, the sound of wheels on the rails kept lulling her to sleep, even though she tried to read. Eventually, she gave up the fight and let her eyes close. *I wonder what it will be like seeing Coll? It's been a long time since I saw him. Email and phone calls just aren't the same as being together.*

Chapter Seven

Laurel stepped lightly from the London train onto the Penzance platform. She moved a few feet from the stream of passengers disembarking behind her and searched the small knot of people waiting to meet the train. Excitement bubbled in her chest as she bounced on her toes looking for Aisling.

"Laurel, over here!" Aisling waved from beside the ticket office at the end of the platform. Before she could wave back, Aisling was racing down the platform, dodging the passengers on their way to the bus station or cab stand. Laurel hurried to meet her as fast as her belongings would let her.

She reached Aisling halfway down the platform and dropped the bags in her hand in order to give her friend a hug. Tears pricked the back of Laurel's eyes. She stepped out of the embrace as Aisling loosened her hold. Self-consciously, she wiped away the moisture on her cheek. Laughing, Aisling did the same.

"What a pair of old grandmothers we are," Ash joked.

"It's so good to be back." Laurel survey the sun drenched scene. She turned back to Ash. "Did you tell Coll I was coming? I didn't mention it to him 'cause I wasn't sure Dad was gonna let me come."

Aisling shook her head, her eyes dancing with mischief. "Not a chance, I want to see the look on his face when he sees you."

"Should I call him, do you think?" Now she was so close to seeing him again she was unaccountably nervous. Maybe he'd changed so much she wouldn't like him anymore, or worse, what if he didn't like her anymore?

"Sure, go on and call him."

"You're sure? We could just go by Emily's and surprise him."

No, better idea. Why don't you call him and pretend you're still at home? Coll has no idea you were planning to come for Christmas."

Laurel slipped the cell phone out of her jacket pocket and tapped Coll's name in the display window. She shifted from foot to foot while it connected. Aisling stood beside her with a huge smile on her face. Finally, the call connected.

"Hallo?" The male voice sounded distracted.

"Hey, Coll. It's me, don't you wish we could share some fish and chips right now?" Laurel repressed the urge to giggle.

"Laurel, is that you, then?"

The voice was more distinct and she figured she had his full attention now.

"Yup, it's me. What are you up to?"

"Nothing much, what about you?"

Laurel frowned, there it was again, that slight hesitation in his voice. What was making him so uneasy, instead of thrilled to hear from her? Conscious of the minutes ticking away on her rather expensive international mobile plan, she decided to do away with the subterfuge and get to the point.

"I'm here Coll, at the train station. In Penzance." She waited for the words which would express his astonishment and joy at her announcement. The silence from the other end of the line forced her to check and see if the connection was dropped. Nope, he should still be there. "Aren't you glad to hear I'm in Penzance?"

"Where did you say you are? You're not really here in Penzance are you?" Laurel could hear excitement warring with something else in his voice.

"I'm at the train station. The *Riviera Express* just arrived about ten minutes ago. Can you come down and pick us up?

"Who is 'us'?" he sounded annoyed.

"Me and Aisling."

"Ash knew you were coming and didn't let on?"

"It was supposed to be a surprise, but then other things happened."

"What other things?"

"Coll, can you just come and pick us up, please? This call is eating up my minutes. I'll explain everything when I see you."

"Does Sarie know you're coming?"

Laurel wrinkled her brow at his tone.

"Yes, she said I was welcome in her house anytime and I worked all summer to save up and come visit for the Christmas holidays." Her voice trembled at bit and she bit her lip.

"I'll ring her and let her know you're here. I'll be down directly to collect you." Coll broke the connection.

"She knew Ash was meeting me," she said quickly, but the connection was already dead.

Laurel shoved the phone back in her pocket and picked up her bags. Ash pushed the bigger suitcase over to a bench by the taxi stand. Laurel shifted from foot to foot and pulled the collar of her oilskin jacket up against the wind which blew sharply across the area. What was Coll's problem? She was so sure he would be excited and happy to see her. Maybe he had second thoughts, maybe he was involved with some other girl and didn't know how to tell her. That would suck royally. Laurel kicked at a crisp wrapper lodged under the edge of the bench.

Perching herself on the wooden bench, she looked at Aisling. At least Ash was happy to see her. "What's up with Coll? He didn't seem happy to find out I was in Penzance. Does he have a girlfriend or something?"

"Not that I know of, but Adelle has the hots for him."

"Who's Adelle? Do I know her?" Laurel searched her memory to try and place the girl.

"Stuart's sister, remember?" Aisling grinned.

"Is he interested in her?" A shard of jealousy speared her.

Aisling laughed and shook her head. "Not hardly. He never talks about anyone except you."

"Then what's he so fired up about, he sounded like he was sorry I came."

"I met your grandmother, did you know that?" Aisling took a step back.

"What! I haven't even seen her yet. Where is she? What does she look like?" Laurel bounced on her toes.

"She looks like she does in that old picture we found in Sarie's books, just a bit more wrinkly. She's staying at Sarie's. I'm supposed to get Coll to drive us all out there. Gort will come with him to pick us up."

"How is Gort? It was horrible what happened to him. His uncle was a real piece of work."

"At least Gort doesn't have to deal with him anymore, the sod.

"I know. It's bad karma to be glad someone's dead, but I just can't help being happy Gort's free of the scumbag." She changed the subject abruptly. "I can't wait to see Gramma Bella. I remember a bit about her, but I was only a kid when she moved off the ranch." Laurel wrinkled her forehead. "What if she doesn't recognize me?"

"I wouldn't worry about that. Sarie told me she sent your gramma some pictures the last time you were in Cornwall. I'm pretty certain she'll know who you are." Aisling pulled her to her feet and picked up one of the bags. "C'mon, let's wait for the lads out by the bus platforms."

Laurel followed behind with the big suitcase. As they reached the white peaked tent-like structures that sheltered the bus platforms, Ash pointed and waved at a small decrepit car just pulling into the pickup area. The Mini was covered in paint splotches of different colours, but the engine hummed evenly.

Gort jumped out of the passenger seat and hugged Laurel tight. "It's just brill to see you again, Laurel. It's grand that you could come. Sarie and Emily can't wait to see you again, and your gramma is running around like an ant on a hot brick."

She returned his embrace and then stepped back to take a better look. "You look great, Gort. And you don't stutter anymore, that's awesome." It was on the tip of her tongue to ask if he'd already met Gramma Bella, too, but Aisling grabbed the bag slung over Laurel's shoulder and heaved it into the car.

"Get a move on. Coll can't stay parked here very long without getting pinched."

Gort took the suitcase and crammed it into the tiny trunk of the car before he and Aisling scrambled into the rear seat. Laurel hesitated on the pavement, suddenly shy now Coll was right in front of her.

"Hurry up," Gort shouted. "We're blocking traffic."

Laurel ducked into the passenger seat beside Coll. "Hey," she greeted him. "Thanks for picking me up." She turned to smile at him. He kept his eyes straight ahead and didn't look at her.

He muttered something in response to her greeting but she couldn't make out what it was.

"Nice to see you again, too." She loaded the words with as much sarcasm as she could muster.

"He's just concentrating on driving, didn't mean to be rude, did you, Coll?" Gort tried to play peacekeeper.

Laurel shook her head and turned her attention to the countryside as they passed the Marazion Marsh and bird sanctuary. The conical shape of Saint Michael's Mount appeared to float on the high tide. Something about the place drew her to it.

"We should make sure to visit Saint Michael's Mount before I leave." Laurel spoke over her shoulder to Ash.

"Agreed, maybe we'll see Corm again," Aisling replied.

"Do you guys know anything about somebody being in trouble? Like I explained on the phone, Ally, Gramma's neighbor, said she was sure someone was in trouble and Gramma was going to help sort it out." Laurel turned as far as the seatbelt would allow so she could look at the passengers in the rear. They were sitting close to each other with their fingers entwined. She smiled and raised an eyebrow at Ash. Her friend grinned back at her.

"Ash can probably answer that better than anyone," Coll said, breaking his silence.

"You remember Gwin Scawen, don't you, Laurel?" Aisling began.

"Of course, I remember him. How is he mixed up in this?"

"Gwin got himself in some kind of trouble, playing tricks on humans that weren't very nice. Actually, they were kind of funny in a mean sort of way, but he never meant no harm by it. Anyway, the Council of Kernow called a meeting and Vear Du went to speak for Gwin. It might have been better if he'd steered well clear of it, 'cause some of the council members have it in for the selkie over something that happened a long time ago."

"Did Gwin get off?" Laurel hated the thought of the little man being punished.

"Gwin did, but Vear Du didn't. They've banished him from interacting with humans. Since a selkie is part seal and part human, sort of, it's a pretty harsh penalty." Ash wiped a tear away.

"What? Does that mean I can't see him? Even if I use the talisman to call him?" Laurel asked.

"I don't know. He might be compelled to answer your call, but if he did, I think it wouldn't go well for him." Gort broke in.

"Who is on this stupid council?" Laurel demanded.

"I don't know them all, only the few that Gwin talks about, and they'll be the ones with little or no power, otherwise he wouldn't even mention their names in front of a mortal."

"Did Gramma have a chance to see him before he was banished?"

"I don't know, you'll have to ask her when you see her," Aisling said.

Laurel settled back in her seat and watched the familiar landmarks flash by as Coll negotiated the narrow lanes leading to Sarie's.

"Are you mad at me about something?" Laurel touched his arm.

Coll glanced over at her, a semblance of a smile twisting his lips.

"I'm not mad at you. It's just weird to have you back."

"Weird, how?"

"You look different, older and … I don't know, just different." He shrugged and let his words trail off.

"You look different too, you know. And you're driving, that's new. You got your license a while ago, I remember you telling me about it. But hearing about it and seeing it are two different things."

"I guess. What about that bloke at home, are you going around with him?" Coll glared at the rear of the car ahead of them.

"You mean Chance? We hang out some, but his sister is usually there, too. I've known them forever. God! It would be like kissing my brother. Gross!" She studied his profile as he drove. The blurred lines of adolescence had matured into the lean hard lines of the adult he would become. A very handsome man, she realized with shock.

"Oh, so you're not going out with him? Why does his Facebook status say he's in a relationship with you?" Coll scowled again.

"Huh, I didn't know that! Well, it's only in his own mind. Believe me."

Coll still didn't seem to be convinced. Laurel turned and caught Aisling's attention and raised her shoulders in a helpless gesture.

"Don't be such a git, mate. Give Laurel a break." Gort reached forward and punched Coll lightly on the arm.

"Bloody hell, I'm driving, you bleeding eejit," Coll snarled.

"Ease up, mate. What's got your knickers in a knot?"

"Can we just call a truce?" Laurel put a hand gently on Coll's forearm and looked at her two friends in the rear seat. "Please? I'm already on pins and needles about seeing Gramma Bella again. I can't deal with you guys fighting and arguing with each other."

Coll grinned ruefully. "Right then, truce," he agreed.

"It's about time," Ash remarked.

"Let's talk about this later, okay?" Laurel spoke to Coll in a low voice.

He nodded and took his eyes off the road long enough to smile at her.

A few minutes later the Mini bounced up the lane to Sarie's house. Laurel leaned forward as they rounded the last curve and the house came into view. It was exactly as she remembered it. "It feels like coming home. I can't wait to see Sarie and Gramma Bella."

Chapter Eight

The Mini was still rolling when Laurel jumped out and made a bee line for the house. She was scarcely down the path when the door burst open and a vaguely familiar woman hurried toward her. Sarie followed behind, her expression a mixture of happiness and concern.

"Laurel! Is it really you? I can't hardly believe it." The woman stopped in front of her and studied Laurel's face. Laurel halted as well, her emotions threatening to overwhelm her, tears pricked the back of her eyes and her breath hitched in her throat. She raised a trembling hand to push a piece of hair behind her ear and swallowed hard.

"Gramma, Gramma Bella? I missed you so much." Fighting back the tears, she threw herself into the woman's open arms.

"My little love, my only granddaughter, I missed you, too," she crooned in her ear.

Bella seemed reluctant to break the embrace. Laurel tried to take a step away, but the embrace only tightened. Sarie cleared her throat. "Let the child get some air, Bella. There'll be plenty of time to get to know her. Just now, I want a hug, too."

Gramma released her, allowing Laurel to hug Sarie. "It's been too long, lovey. My word, you've grown up so much. You look like a young lady now instead of a little girl." The older woman held her at arms' length and the heat rose in Laurel's face under the scrutiny. "Come in the house and have a cuppa. The tea's steeping and we can have a good natter."

"It's good to be back," Laurel glanced around, "and it is so amazing to see you again, Gramma. I thought you were dead."

“Why on earth would you think that, child?” Bella appeared stunned.

“Dad and Mom let me believe it. You disappeared so fast, one day you were there, and then you were gone. They were both upset and Mom kept crying when she thought I wasn’t around. Dad said you’d gone away to live in a better place. That’s what they told me when my old barn cat died. I was only a little kid, so I never questioned it. Why did you never try to get in touch with me?”

“I promised your father I wouldn’t. A promise I’ve lived to regret bitterly.”

“Let’s go in and enjoy our cuppa. Come along, Bella, you and Laurel can catch up inside,” Sarie urged.

“Where do you want the suitcase?” Coll dragged the large suitcase up the path. Gort and Aisling trailed behind laden down with the rest of her stuff.

“In the spare room at the top of the stairs, across from the one Laurel had last time, please Coll,” Sarie said. “You can put the rest of her things there too.” She nodded at Gort and Aisling.

“Thanks you guys, but really I can cart them upstairs myself,” Laurel protested.

“No worries, glad to do it. You go spend some time with your gramma, just save some cream tea for me.” Gort grinned at her as he went past on the narrow path.

“Cream tea? Yummy, let’s go,” Laurel exclaimed. With Sarie on one side and Bella on the other holding her hand they headed for the front door. Almost before she could blink, Laurel was sitting at the table with a mug of tea in front of her. Coll, Gort, and Aisling pushed through the door from the hall into the kitchen. The old Aga stove radiated a welcome warmth. It was just like old times.

Coll slid into the chair beside Laurel, who caught the amused look that passed between Gort and Aisling. Gramma took the chair across from her. Laurel glanced at Coll when his leg bumped against hers under the table. She was grasping for the right words to say when Bella interrupted her thoughts.

"I suppose you want to know what your dad and I fought over all those years ago," she said.

"I imagine it was when he found out Grampa D'Arcy wasn't his real father," Laurel said bluntly.

Bella gasped, all the colour leaching from her face. "I didn't realize you knew that." Her voice was thin as if she couldn't get enough breath to speak at a normal volume. "Did Anna tell you?"

"No, Vear Du told me," Laurel informed her.

"When was that? When you were here last, when Anna was so sick?"

Laurel nodded, dismayed by the tears coursing down Bella's cheeks.

Sarie laid a comforting hand on her friend's shoulder.

"Does your father know you discovered my secret?"

"Not a chance, he'd go ballistic. Mom knows though, I told her what I found out when I was here last time."

Coll's hand curled around hers under the table. Laurel glanced at him and tightened her fingers around his.

"I met Ally, your neighbor in Bragg Creek. Chance drove me up there to find you. She said you left in a hurry and you were upset. Who is in trouble?" Laurel steered the conversation away from her dad. "Is it Vear Du? Ally said you kept muttering 'oh dear, oh, dear' but I'm pretty sure you meant Vear. Am I right?"

Laurel jumped, her pulse racing as a small disembodied voice interrupted whatever Bella was planning to say.

"'Tis all my fault, so it is. No one can tell me different." Gwin Scawen materialized out of thin air, sitting cross legged on the table in front of Aisling.

"Gwin Scawen! Hi, it's great to see you," Laurel greeted the piskie.

"Hello, Mistress Laurel. It's good to see you back in Kernow."

"What is your fault, what are you talking about?" Laurel asked.

"It's not really his fault, although he did set the wheels in motion. In the end, the blame rests on the Council," Aisling replied.

"Not all of them, just a few, but enough to influence the vote," Sarie said.

"It's not fair, I'm sure that old witch pressured the weaker members to vote with her." Ash was vehement, her eyes flashing with anger.

"Oh, do be careful, Mistress Aisling, my flower. The one you speak of has spies everywhere. You don't want to bring her wrath down on your head," Gwin Scawen whispered.

"I'm not afraid of her," Aisling declared.

"Who are you talking about, what council?" Laurel interrupted.

"Maybe you should explain, Bella, seeing as you've had to stand before them in the past," Sarie said.

"It's not a memory I like to dwell on. But I'll explain it the best I can," Bella agreed.

She took Laurel's hand and smiled at her across the table. Coll tightened his grip on the fingers of Laurel's other hand.

"I don't like the sounds of this at all," he muttered.

"Be quiet," Laurel hissed at him.

"You should all be well aware, after your adventures last time, that there's a parallel world that co-exists alongside the one we know. There are those who can slip between the veils that separate us by simply concentrating and taking a step sideways. Everyone at this table is capable of that feat. Creatures and things of magic exist there. It is where most of the legends and myths of the area were born. In order to keep some semblance of balance and keep the inhabitants of that place from wreaking havoc on the mortals, The Council of Elders was formed." Bella paused and looked at Laurel. "Each region has a Council, our local one is the Council of Kernow, and there is a Grand Council that oversees it all."

"Who is on this council thing?" Gort interjected.

"The Selkie king and queen, the Mermaid of Padstow, Cormoran and Bottrell for the Giants, Bucca Gwidden and Buca Dhu represent the Knockers, Pobel Vean stands for the rest of the Piskies, the Witches of Logan Rock send a representative when Council is convened. They only assemble when something has gone seriously wrong, something which endangers the balance between the worlds."

"What did you do?" Coll demanded of Gwin.

"T'was only a small matter, so it t'was, Master Coll." The leathery little brown man wrung his hands together.

"Or so you thought." Sarie favoured him with a stern stare. "You caused all kinds of a ruckus, and now someone else is paying the piper instead of you."

"I know, I know," he wailed.

"What did he do?" Laurel ignored the piskie who was blubbering on Aisling's shoulder.

"He thought maybe it would be a good idea to have a piskie hooley down at the Jubilee Pool in Penzance. Invited everyone he knew, and they invited everyone they knew. At some point the revelry got a little out of hand and they started playing pranks on the humans who were there, all unawares that there was a host of piskies underfoot. It went from tipping over tables and chairs to tossing towels into the water. Then someone had the brill idea to allow the humans to see them. They pretty much violated all the rules The Council has mandated." Sarie scowled at the little man who burrowed his face deeper in Aisling's shoulder.

"It just sounds like fairly harmless fun," Laurel defended Gwin.

"Oh, it was only meant in fun, I grant you that. But in all the confusion, a child almost drowned. Got knocked into the water by a bunch of ill-mannered piskies who should never have been there. Those Red Caps are always trouble," Sarie said.

"Is the kid okay?" Laurel asked.

"Last I heard he was doing fine, still in the hospital in town here."

"How did Vear Du get mixed up in it," Gort asked.

"He showed up when Gwin here called for assistance in saving the boy and controlling the mob of little men and women who were fixing to rampage all over Penzance creating as much havoc as possible," Sarie replied.

"So he saved the kid from drowning and scared off the Red Caps, what's so bad about that?" A frown creased Gort's forehead.

"Vear Du used magic to save the child. Something he is forbidden to do in the presence of mortals. It was his second offence and The Council didn't take kindly to his actions. To them one human more or less isn't a matter for concern." Sarie raised her shoulders helplessly and glanced at Bella.

"You don't need to look at me like that, Sarie! I know I was the cause of his first transgression all that time ago when we were young," Bella declared.

"Anyway, Gwin got hauled up before the Kernow Council and got raked over the coals, but the real target of their wrath was Vear Du." Sarie shook her head. "There's been bad blood between him and some of the local Council ever since he and Bella got together. They've just been waiting for him to take a wrong step so they could pounce on it as an excuse to banish him."

"What so they mean by banish, exactly? Where did they send him?" Ash stroked Gwin's shoulder and the little man pulled a hanky out of his pocket and blew his long nose with a great deal of honking.

"It means he can no longer interact with humans. The king and queen of Selkies are also angry with him, so he is not welcome in their community either. It is a sore, sad place they have put him in," Gwin said morosely.

"Did you get to see him before this happened?" Laurel touched Bella's hand.

"Just once, for a very short time. He must have anticipated how the Council meeting would go. He told me to meet him at Nanjizal on the next new moon. His friend Treagle is always there doomed to fill the bay with sand only to have it washed away again. Treagle has promised to create a diversion of some kind so I can slip through the cleft and be with Vear. I'm not sure how long I will be able to stay, but I haven't come this far to not straighten things out between us," Bella replied.

"I could help," Gwin spoke up.

"Best you lie low. We may need you to speak to Pobel Vean on Vear's behalf if his request for an appeal is granted. He's going to need all the support he can get," Sarie said.

"Aye, he will that," Gwin agreed.

"What can we do to help?" Laurel and Aisling spoke at the same time.

"Nothing right now. It is a shame that Vear and Bella are parted again now that she's back in Penzance," Sarie said.

"I never should have left, I should have defied Da and stayed right here. He had to be mental to think I would ever marry Daniel Treliving." Bella shivered with disgust.

"Daniel…my Uncle Daniel?" Gort was aghast at the idea.

"Yes, that Daniel. Da knew the man wanted to marry me no matter what the gossips said. No respectable man would ask for me after the scandal of me running away and then turning up pregnant a few months later." Bella's face twisted in a grimace.

"I'm glad you didn't have anything to do with that man," Laurel said.

"At the time it seemed like the only path open to me was to agree to Da's wishes and accept an arranged marriage with a homesteader in the wilds of Canada. That was your Grampa D'Arcy, dear." She smiled at Laurel. "He was a good man and never held it against me that he got two for the price of one in the bargain."

"No wonder Dad was so angry. You should have told him right from the start," Laurel declared.

"What was I to tell him? Oh, by the way, your father is some mythical shape shifter who doesn't even know of your existence? No, I let the hare sit and let him believe D'Arcy was his father. In every way that counted, he was. D'Arcy loved Colton and treated him as if he were his birth father. He was a good, kind, forgiving man and I couldn't bring myself to break either of their hearts."

"You still should have told him when he was old enough to understand," Laurel maintained stubbornly.

"Perhaps you're right, Laurel. I just didn't have the courage. Just like I didn't have the courage to stay here in Cornwall, or to tell Vear that somehow we had conceived a child together."

"He knows now," Coll said.

"How could he?" Bella gasped and her hand flew to her throat.

'I told him last time I was here. He knows I'm his granddaughter and that Dad is his son," Laurel said defiantly.

"Oh, my stars." Bella's face crumpled up with tears.

"Leave off, Bella. You knew it had to come out when you decided to come back here," Sarie said.

"I suppose I did." She sniffed.

Gwin Scawen moved from Aisling's lap to sit on the edge of the table, his thin legs swinging as if dancing to a tune only he could hear. He cocked his head to the side for a moment and then jumped to his feet. "I'm off to keep company with the big black one, is there any message you wish me to carry to him?"

"Please tell him I'm here," Laurel said.

"Tell him I plan to be where Treagle toils at the dark of the moon," Bella said.

"I will do that, Mistress Bella and Mistress Laurel." He tipped his pointed hat to them in turn. "It warms the cockles of my heart to see you back on Cornish soil." Gwin grinned at Aisling before vanishing with a soft sound of displaced air.

Chapter Nine

After the piskie left, the conversation turned to more mundane things. Sarie and Bella had their heads together speaking too low for Laurel to hear. Coll tugged on her hand to catch her attention and nodded toward the door. Laurel smiled and stood up at the same time he did. Aisling looked up in surprise and left off whatever she and Gort had been discussing.

"Where are you going?"

"Just outside, so Laurel can see the changes since she left," Coll said.

"To visit the horses," Laurel said at the same time.

Gort laughed and waved a hand toward the door. "It's been a long time since you saw each other, go on with you and have a good natter in private."

Coll held the door out into the mudroom open for Laurel before following her out of the kitchen. He opened the outer door and followed her out, snibbing the latch firmly behind him. He took Laurel's hand and they wandered down the well-worn path toward Sarie's herb garden. There were still a few hardy patches of green among the rows. Laurel was content to walk through the familiar surroundings without speaking, noticing the minor changes since her last visit. Coll seemed equally happy to keep her company.

"Are you going out with someone back home, other than that Chance chap?

Coll's sudden question startled Laurel out of her thoughts. She stopped walking and turned to face him. "No, not really," she said slowly.

“You sure? You said you’re just friends, but you’re always blethering on about Chance did this or Chance said that.” Coll’s face flushed a deep red.

“Of course, I talk about him, he’s Carly’s brother so of course we end up doing things together. He’s like my brother.” Laurel decided not to mention the fact Chance wanted to be more than friends.

“If you’re sure, then.” Coll released her hand and stepped closer, putting both arms around her waist. Her breath caught in her throat and she forgot to breathe, staring at the golden flecks in his hazel eyes. His lips brushed hers lightly, and when she didn’t object, he deepened the kiss. Laurel sighed when he lifted his head and she leaned her cheek on his chest. It wasn’t like she’d never kissed a guy, but none of those encounters had affected her this way. Coll’s heart sounded like a trip hammer in her ear and her own heart seemed to be racing.

“C’mon, let’s go see the ponies.” Coll broke the silence. Laurel removed her arms from around his shoulders, surprised she didn’t remember putting them there in the first place.

“Sure, I want to see Lamorna and all of them.”

Coll caught her hand and stopped her as she moved away. “I really missed you, Laurel.” He pulled her into his arms and kissed her again. Her whole body felt flushed and she leaned into Coll to support her trembling legs. After a moment he lifted his head, and leaving an arm around her shoulders, walked beside her down to the pony field. Laurel couldn’t keep from smiling, she’d often thought about kissing Coll, but the reality far outshone her expectations.

“I missed you too, Coll. More than I can say.”

She rested her elbows on the top rail of the gate, close enough to Coll that her hip was in contact with his. A tiny thrill of an emotion she couldn’t quite name ran through her. Putting her fingers to her lips, she whistled shrilly. Coll jumped at the sound and tightened his arm around her shoulder.

“I forgot you could whistle like that.” He grinned down at her.

Laurel slipped her own arm about his waist and hooked her thumb in one of his belt loops. She'd seen the older girls at the rodeo do that and suddenly felt very grown up and daring.

The four black ponies and the two big mares came galloping up the field and slid to a stop by the gate. Lamorna stuck her velvety nose into Laurel's hand looking for a treat. She stroked the pony's nose and straightened the thick forelock that fell over the large expressive eyes.

"Hey, pretty mare. I don't have anything for you right now. I promise I'll come back later with some horse nuts for you."

She removed her arm from Coll's waist and he released her as well and turned to lean a hip on the fence. She glanced at him and found him studying her with a thoughtful expression on his face. Bright blue eyes peering at her through the blonde hair falling over his forehead.

"What's it like, seeing your gramma again? Is she like you remember her?"

"It's great she's here." Laurel paused and frowned. "But it's weird, too. I was so little when she left I don't remember how she looked. I just remember bits of things, how she smelled of lavender, baking cookies with her…that kind of thing. I really hope I have a chance to get to know her."

Coll shook his head. "I can't imagine not seeing my gramma every day."

"But Emily raised you. It would be more like how it would be if you could see your parents again. You probably don't remember much about them, do you?"

"No, not very much. Just unconnected flashes of things. I have to keep looking at the photos Gramma has of them to even be able to remember what they looked like."

"Sometimes life just sucks," Laurel exclaimed and turned her gaze back to the horses.

"Laurel! Coll!" Sarie's voice carried clearly in the still air.

"Coming," Laurel called back.

After one last caress of Lamorna's neck, she started back to the house. Coll caught up to her and twined his fingers with hers. She smiled up at him and suddenly felt light as a feather.

"How did you get to Bragg Creek to find out where your gramma was? I thought you said it was a fair drive from where you live." A small frown furrowed Coll's brow.

"Chance took me," she admitted.

"Oh. Did your friend Carly go with you? You haven't mentioned her."

"No. Just me and Chance. Why?" Laurel stopped walking and he halted beside her.

"No reason…I guess I thought you'd take your girlfriend with you…" His voice trailed off and a deep flush darkened his fair complexion.

"Are you jealous of Chance?" Laurel found the idea astounding. "I told you he's only a friend. I've known him forever. He's like my big brother or something, you idiot." She punched him on the arm with her free hand.

Coll let out a big sigh and the frown disappeared. "Good to know. I haven't gone out with anyone since you left. Did you realize that?"

"Ash told me. I haven't dated anyone either, just so you know. Even if one of us did date someone else, it's not like we made a pact or anything. You could have seen another girl while I was gone." Laurel pointed out the obvious.

"Are you saying that because you did go out with someone when you were home?" His jaw clenched and he looked away from her.

"No, you jackass! I just said I didn't."

Coll's face contorted in a strange rictus and it took Laurel a moment to realize he was trying not to laugh.

"What's so funny?"

"Jackass," he spluttered, half speaking and half laughing. "Jackass," he said again and pulled her close again. "Come on, we'd better get a move on, the others are waiting for us.

Laurel let him steer her onto the path through the vegetable garden that led to the back door. *What's so funny about with jackass? Dad says that all the time.*

The mood was sombre when they entered the kitchen. Sarie sat across from Bella with a worried frown on her face. Bella's expression reminded Laurel of her dad when he had his mind set on something and nothing short of a stampede would make him budge. *What are they arguing about?* She released Coll's hand and slid into the chair beside Aisling. "What's up?" she whispered.

Bella plans to hike out to Nanjizal when the tide is out and use that narrow cleft in the rock as a portal. Sarie thinks she should wait and see if Vear Du contacts her first. She's worried that Bella will get lost or maybe end up in the wrong place on the other side," Ash whispered back.

"What do you think? Can Gwin go with her as a guide?"

"Maybe…he's so scared of the 'big un's' as he calls them, I'm not sure he'll do it, no matter how much he cares for your gramma."

Laurel shifted forward on her chair and Vear Du's talisman dug into her buttock. She reached back and pulled it from the back pocket of her jeans. It sparkled momentarily in the overhead light.

"You shouldn't chance it, Bella. Not without some idea of where you're going. And, if you don't find him, do you have a plan to get yourself back to this side?" Sarie continued the argument.

"I don't have a plan, but I'm sure I can find Vear and he'll know how to get back. You just worry too much, Sarie. Just like when we were young," Bella said belligerently.

"Just look how that turned out," Sarie shot back.

"It turned out pretty well, if you ask me." Bella tipped her chin in Laurel's direction.

"But not without a lot of pain and heartbreak. You're still just a stubborn and hard headed as you were when we were young. How can you be so blind?" Sarie's face was set in stern lines.

“You could have my talisman that Vear Du gave me up on the Cheesewring. It got us in and out of the caverns under Glastonbury Tor.” Laurel dangled the cowrie shell attached to the leather cord from her fingers. “I think it will work for you as well as did for me.”

Sarie and Bella turned their attention to her, the argument momentarily forgotten.

“It might work.” Sarie looked thoughtful. “You’re both of the same bloodline, although it’s strongest in Laurel as she carries both your blood and Vear’s.”

“Can I hold it, Laurel?” Bella held out her hand palm up.

She reached across and placed the item in Gramma Bella’s hand. The air shimmered over it and the thong appeared to twist itself around her fingers. “It might just work,” Bella whispered.

“But what if it doesn’t?” Sarie persisted.

“It’s the best chance I’ve got. Don’t forget he’ll be looking for me, too. I bet he’s just standing there waiting for me when I step though.”

“Is there some way to find out what will happen?” Gort spoke for the first time in a long while.

“I don’t think so—,” Bella began.

“Yes, there just might be. Gort, you’re a genius,” Sarie interrupted her.

“How?” Coll sounded dubious.

Laurel grinned, he was always the last one to come around and acknowledge that the magic was real.

“I can perform a Teinmlaide…” she paused for a moment, “It’s not too long after Samhain and Alban Arthuran is coming soon. It might give us some idea of what to expect and how much of a chance there is of Bella succeeding in meeting up with Vear.”

“What is that? A Ten…” Aisling stumbled over the strange word. Her eyes sparkled with interest and anticipation. She loved learning about magic and esoteric things.

“It’s a ritual where a person prepares themselves and asks a question. The answer is given by symbols or sigils in the language of the ogham,” Sarie replied.

“Can we watch?” Gort wanted to know.

“Can I help?” Aisling chimed in.

“How do you perform the ritual?” Laurel leaned forward.

Coll sat back in his chair and shook his head. Sarie made him uncomfortable sometimes, the air shimmered and felt heavy with unseen power whenever she did magic.

“First off, Gort, yes you can watch the ritual, but you must remain silent and promise never to break the circle I cast. No, Aisling, there is nothing you can do to help during the actual ritual, but you can help me prepare my tools if you like. You too, Laurel, if you want to.”

“What about me, what should I do?” Bella leaned across and took Sarie’s hand.

“You, my dear, may sit outside the circle and hold the thought of you and Vear Du together in the other worlds.”

“I can do that,” she agreed. “How soon can it be done?”

“The day after tomorrow. I need to prepare myself and the tools I require must be charged with my intent. Don’t frown at me, Bella. The new moon is still a few days away. You can’t go until then anyway.”

“Come with me, girls. We can start by assembling the things we will need.”

Laurel and Aisling hurried to follow her out into the mud room where Sarie opened a door Laurel had never noticed before. They crowded in behind Sarie. The room was redolent with the tang of drying herbs, bunches of which hung from the beams of the ceiling. Sarie opened a drawer in a small chest and pulled out a leather bag, along with a short knife with an ornately carved handle. She laid the items on the work bench by the long window and added a bottle of water marked *Water from the White Lady’s Spring.* A bundle of herbs wrapped with red thread came next. Sarie paused beside a cabinet filled with small drawers, each one labelled with the name of a tree.

“Let me see, which is best…” Sarie muttered as if talking to herself. “Birch perhaps, for new beginnings? No, I don’t think so. Yew for rebirth? No, no, that doesn’t feel right either.” She opened the drawers of each wood she mentioned and ran her fingers down the staves enclosed there. "Oak, maybe, for protection, or Holly to be the best in a fight…ahhh, here we are. Ash, I think, yes, Ash will do. Inner and outer worlds linked." She withdrew two staves from the drawer marked with a straight vertical line with five short horizontal lines sticking out from it on the right side of the vertical line.

She appeared to have forgotten that Laurel and Aisling were with her, all her attention focused inward. Opening a tall cupboard, she pulled out a cloak embroidered with sigils and signs Laurel didn't recognize. Sarie shook the creases from the cloak and hung it so the light from the setting sun shone on it. Next, she pulled a loose gown of the same material from the cupboard and hung it beside the cloak. The last item she added to the pile on the table was a brass bowl, shining with the patina of long use. Nodding her head, she turned back to the two girls.

"There, that will do for now. I'll explain what everything is for when the time comes. For now, let's go back and join the others for a cuppa."

Laurel would rather have asked about the symbols on the cloak. Something about them intrigued her, as if she should know what they meant. She trailed after the others into the kitchen where Sarie was putting the kettle on the hob to make tea.

Chapter Ten

After everyone else had left, Laurel and her grandmother stayed in the kitchen while Sarie went to her room. "I need some time alone to prepare for the Tienmlaida tomorrow," she explained.

"Are you excited about seeing Vear Du again?" Laurel asked.

"Excited and scared," Bella admitted. "But let's talk about you, my little love. It's so wonderful to see you again. The last time I saw you, you were still a little girl."

"I remember you, though. You used to let me help bake cookies and you'd tell me the names of all the flowers in the garden."

"Do you, now?" Bella smiled. "I wasn't sure you'd recall anything at all. You were only…what…six years old when I left?"

"I was six. I remember asking where you were and Mom and Dad said you'd gone away and couldn't come back. I thought you had gone to heaven because that's what they said about Snooksie, my cat, when she died. I never knew you were still alive until I came over here and found the letters you wrote to Sarie."

"Is your father still as dead set against me as he was?" A hopeful light shone in Bella's eyes.

"He won't even mention your name. I didn't tell him I was going to Bragg Creek to look for you, or he would've grounded me. Mom knew, though," Laurel said.

"If Vear Du is his father…does that mean Dad can shape shift, too? I mean, is it possible he can do magic, real magic?" She studied her nails and peeked at Bella out of the corner of her eye.

"I don't rightly know, sweetie. I suppose it's possible he could, but he's put up such a wall between himself and even the thought of magic he may have buried it too deep in his psyche for it ever to manifest itself." Bella patted her hand.

"Am I magic too?" Laurel voiced the thought that had been lurking at the back of her mind ever since she found out about the selkie and her grandmother.

"Now that's a thought." Bella sounded surprised. "It explains why the fire salamander, Belerion, came to your aid, and your ability to communicate with the White Lady of the spring. It's why your friend Aisling is such a favourite of that scamp Gwin Scawen."

"Ash is magic?" Laurel stared at Gramma Bella. "How, it's not through her mom, she hates anything to do with magic, or anything out of the ordinary."

"Alice Nuin is very much like my Colton. Her grandmother, Aisling's great grandmother, was fey. She taught Sarie a lot of what she knows about herbs and healing. Morwenna was a well-respected hedge witch. She also told fortunes and read the tarot cards. Alice was afraid of her. I remember when we were in school the boys would tease her about her grandmother. I don't know what happened to make Alice so scared, but she wouldn't even attend the bonfires on Guy Fawkes Night or any of the old celebrations. She's closed her mind to everything that isn't solid and real, just like your dad."

"That's so sad, though. Seeing Belerion and Gwin Scawen and everything is really cool. Mom used to tell me stories when I was a kid about undines, and gnomes, and stuff. But never when Dad was around."

"Your mother is a very special person. Colton couldn't have picked a better wife." Bella smiled and looked over Laurel's head into the middle distance.

"Yeah, she's pretty cool. Did you know she came to stand up for me when I was bargaining with Gwin ap Nudd inside Glastonbury Tor? She put him in his place pretty quick." Laurel grinned at the memory.

"You'll have to tell me that story sometime soon. But now we should get to bed. Morning comes early and I think Sarie plans to start at dawn, just before sunrise." Bella rose and checked the fire in the Aga stove to be sure it would last until morning.

Laurel got up and followed her down the narrow dark hallway to the foot of the stairs. Bella stopped and hugged her. "I'm so happy you're here. I love you, sweetie."

"I love you, too, Gramma." Laurel burrowed her head into Bella's shoulder and inhaled the sharp lavender scent she always associated with her gramma.

* * *

Laurel woke up when she heard Sarie stirring in the room down the hall. She threw back the covers and dressed hurriedly in the early morning chill. There was certainly something to be said for central heat, she mused while pulling thick socks onto her cold feet. By the time she reached the kitchen Sarie was already outside. Gramma Bella handed Laurel a mug of hot chocolate and led the way out into the pre-dawn gloom. Pale bands of yellow lightened the eastern sky.

Bella led the way through an arched doorway at the end of the herb garden. Laurel had never gone through there before, Sarie had always taken care of it herself, and Laurel had never given it much thought. Sarie stood in the centre of a grassy open space, a bowl of spring water on the ground by her feet. Bella motioned toward a wooden bench at the side of the gate. Bella sat beside her and took her hand.

Sarie took the two sticks she chose the night before and laid them near the centre of the circle. She placed the ornately carved knife beside them. A silky, deep blue scarf was laid across them. She sprinkled them with water from the brass bowl three times. She turned to face the east and picked up the blue scarf and placed it around her shoulders.

Laurel leaned forward to see better when Sarie picked up the two sticks and held one in either hand. She began to speak in a sing-song voice:

I stand today by
The strength of heaven
Light of sun
Radiance of moon
Splendour of fire
Speed of lightening
Swiftness of wind
Kindness of rain
Might of the sea
Firmness of earth
Stability of rock

I am guarded,
Guided,
Shielded and blessed,
By the three that are above me
By the three that are below me
By the three that are over me
By the three that are under me
By the three that are before me
By the three that are behind me
By the three on my right hand
By the three on my left hand
By the three that are within me

By the nine threes am I standing
By the nine threes am I seeing
By the nine threes am I singing

There was more, but Sarie's voice dropped and Laurel couldn't make out the words. Sarie stood motionless, her eyes closed, for what seemed like a long time. She glanced at her grandmother. Bella leaned forward, watching the still figure intently. The sky brightened as the minutes passed, a small slice of brilliant orange flaring on the horizon. A slender beam of light seemed to pierce the center of the small garden, connecting Sarie with the glory of the rising sun. A moment later, Sarie opened her eyes and looked straight ahead.

"I see the red of rowan berry, protection from enchantment. I see acorns of the oak, protection and doorway to the mysteries. I see the dark yew, symbol of rebirth and everlasting life," Sarie repeated the words three times. She sat on the dew wet grass as the sun swung free of the curve of the earth, flooding the tiny garden with light. Picking up one of the sticks, she made some marks on it with the ornate knife. She carved three symbols, but Laurel couldn't tell if she was making three different marks or repeating the same one over and over. She laid the first piece on the ground and took up the second one. Her hand moved deftly, carving a number of symbols into the soft wood. Sarie laid the sticks on the grass in front of her and stared at them intently. The sun had risen a hand's span into the sky before she moved and picked up the first stick again and began to carve more marks. Picking up the second stick, Sarie rose to her feet and stood in the full light of the morning sun.

"I see a journey into an enchanted land, with much danger to the travellers. I see a door cracked open at the end of a perilous path. I see a life reborn, but shadowed with sorrow that burns away in the brilliant light of love." She repeated the words three times.

Laurel frowned and leaned close to her grandmother. "What does she mean?" she whispered.

Bella shook her head and held a finger to her lips.

Sarie finished the last of the ritual and placed the carved sticks on the grass. She took up the brass bowl and blessed the four directions starting in the north. Laying the bowl back on the grass she removed the scarf and placed it over the bowl and sticks. She startled Laurel by clapping her hands sharply three times.

"The circle is open,
But ever unbroken,
This ritual is complete," she declared.

Gathering up the regalia she used in the ritual, she turned and smiled at Laurel. “Well, that’s that. Let’s go have some breakfast, I’m starved.”

Laurel walked beside her grandmother following Sarie into the house. Bella put the kettle on the stove to heat and Laurel got out mugs and the makings for breakfast. Sarie disappeared up the stairs to store her ritual items safely away. She reappeared a few minutes later and sat at the table regarding Bella thoughtfully. Laurel put a plate of toast in front of her along with a pot of preserves. Her gramma carried the big pottery tea pot over to the table and joined them. After Sarie was finished eating, Bella cleared the dishes away.

Laurel was dying to ask what Sarie had discovered from the dawn ceremony. The carvings fascinated her and she stared at the two sticks lying on the table by Sarie’s plate. Although she could make no sense out of the markings, there did seem to be an underlying thread connecting them. *I guess if I couldn’t read English the alphabet wouldn’t make sense to me either.*

“What did you find out?” Bella stood up and moved restlessly around the room picking things up and putting them down again at random.

“Sit down, Bella. You’re running around like a fly on a hot brick,” Sarie declared.

“I can’t help it. I have the most awful feeling that time is running out for Vear. I need to go and speak with him and see if there is something I can do to help. It’s been so long…I just really need to see him.”

Laurel swallowed at the bright sheen of unshed tears in her grandmother’s blue eyes. “It’ll be okay, Gramma. I know it will.”

“Sit down, Bella. Listen to what I have to say.” Sarie waved at the empty chair beside her. “First, I agree you should try and contact the selkie, meet him at Nanjizal like he asked. The augury is fairly positive, although it does show the possibility of certain danger. It appears that things will work out in your favour in the end. But remember that nothing is certain when it concerns the future, Bella." Sarie cautioned her friend.

"I'm going to pack some things and go out to the bay today." Bella dashed out the hall door before Sarie could say anything more. Laurel glanced at the ceiling at the sound of her footsteps echoing overhead.

"I see she hasn't got any wiser in her old age," Sarie remarked dryly.

"What do mean?" Laurel bristled at the implied criticism of her grandmother.

"Don't look at me like that, young lady. Bella never had any patience when we were girls, her impulsiveness always got us into trouble," Sarie said.

"Okay, so what do you think we should do?" Laurel said.

"You should do nothing. Bella and I will go out to the old ring fort at Carn les Boel and then down into Nanjizal bay. If Vear is there as planned, Bella can speak with him and maybe things will be clearer then."

"I'm going with you!" There was no way Laurel was staying at home when all the excitement was playing out on the sands of Nanjizal. "If you don't take me I'll just follow you on my own."

"It's way too far for you to walk there." Sarie stuck to her guns.

"Coll can drive. He'll take me if I ask him. You know he will," Laurel pushed her advantage.

Sarie's shoulders sagged in defeat. "He would too, the wee rascal. You can come with us, but you are to stay far away from the portal, do you understand?"

Laurel nodded. "Aisling and the boys will want to come too, you know. Gort might even be able to help out because he can ask GogMagog if he knows what's going on."

Sarie's expression brightened. "I almost forgot about that spirit stallion of his. He might come in very useful. Go give them a ring and ask them to be here by four in the afternoon when the tide is on the way out. We should be at the bay when the tide is at its lowest ebb."

With a squeal of delight, Laurel jumped up to ring Aisling who promised to get in touch with Gort and ask him to see what Gog thought about things. Laurel wanted to contact Coll herself. She wiped her sweaty palm on her jeans and waited for the butterflies in her stomach to settle before she rang Emily's number. Coll answered and agreed to bring Gort and Aisling with him later in the afternoon. After hanging up, Laurel left Gramma Bella and Sarie sorting through things upstairs and wandered outside. Stopping by the pony field, she leaned on the fence and waited for the horses to come over. She stroked Lamorna's neck and spoke to the sturdy pony standing beside the mare. He'd appeared with Gort at the Men an Tol when they returned from the crystal caves under Glastonbury Tor. Gort explained it was how his *anam cara*, his soul friend, appeared in the everyday world. When they entered the other worlds the horse's true self was revealed. It was hard to reconcile the shaggy pony and his huge expressive eyes with the crystalline magnificence of the stallion that made his home with his brethren under the Tor. Sometimes Laurel thought she'd dreamed the whole thing up, but Mom was healthy now and the doctors said it was a miracle the cancer was in remission.

"So, Gog, what do you think of all this?" she addressed the solemn pony.

He shook his head and snorted before pawing the earth. He turned and took a few paces toward the small valley that bisected the field. He stopped and looked back over his shoulder at her and whickered. When she stayed where she was, he took another few steps and stopped again, tossing his head as he looked back at her.

"You want me to follow you?" Laurel used the fence as an aid and slid onto Lamorna's wide back. She nudged the pony with her heels and set off across the springy grass, following Gog's broad hind end. When they reached the narrow path down into the hollow, she swung her leg over Lamorna's back and landed lightly on the ground. Gog disappeared around the first bend and Laurel hurried to catch up.

“We’re going to the spring, aren’t we?” She walked behind the pony until they reached the small stream that cascaded down the steep side of the valley. The pony halted and moved aside. He pushed Laurel with his nose toward the top of the series of waterfalls. “Okay, okay, I’m going.” She laughed at him. Gog whickered deep in his throat and for a moment the image of the tall silvery stallion wavered in the soft shadows of the trees. Laurel started up the side of the stream. Memories of the last time she’d come this way came unbidden to her mind. At the top of the series of waterfalls was a hidden pool overhung with ferns and sheltered by tall trees. It was where she’d met the White Lady and set off on the quest to heal her mother. She crossed her fingers and hoped Gramma Bella’s adventure would turn out well.

Chapter Eleven

The small glade with the pool of clear water in the centre was the same as she remembered. Sunlight fell through the leaves and dappled the still surface of the water. Laurel sat cross legged on the flat stone by the edge of the pool and closed her eyes. She tried to empty her mind of any thoughts, but things kept popping up as quickly as she pushed them away. The rustle of cloth and a touch on her shoulder startled Laurel. She gasped and opened her eyes. The Lady stood beside Laurel, her long silver-blonde hair shimmering in the green-gold light of the glade.

"Greetings to you, Laurel the seeker," her musical voice reminded Laurel of tiny bells chiming in the wind.

"Hello." Laurel didn't know what else to say.

"What is it you seek this time? I can't promise to help, but help I will if I can." She inclined her head gracefully.

"I'm not sure…GogMagog brought me here, but I don't know why," she admitted.

"Does it concern the selkie known as Vear Du and the human woman he loves?" The Lady tilted her head to one side, a small frown furrowing her beautiful face.

"She's my grandmother, the person Vear Du loves. She loves him, too."

"Love between mortals and immortals is always fraught with strife, and generally ends in heartbreak," her voice mingled with the sound of the water tumbling over the rocks below the pool.

"Is there a chance they can be happy? They've been separated for so long and it just doesn't seem fair," Laurel implored her.

"It may seem like a long time to you, but for us it is only a fleeting moment. Think on it, human child. The mortal woman may ache for her lover for a few decades, but the immortal who has given his heart to her will endure centuries and eons of that longing," the Lady's voice faded away and her silvery eyes clouded with sorrow.

"Isn't there some way they can be together?" Tears pricked the back of Laurel's eyes.

"Not that I am aware of." The Lady laid her hand on Laurel's head. "There is one who might know more, he is far older than most of us. He was here when Kernow came into being all those eons ago."

"Who is it?" Laurel scrambled to her feet. "Where can I find him?"

"He is on the moor near the Men an Tol. You remember where that is, do you not?"

"Of course I do. But there's nothing out there other than the Lanyon Tea House. Does he live there?"

Silvery laughter filled the glade as the breeze fluttered the leaves on the trees. "No, dear child. He does not live within the flimsy confines of man-made contrivances."

Laurel didn't find anything funny about the situation. If this person could help Gramma Bella and the selkie be together she needed to find him sooner rather than later.

"Don't frown so, daughter of Eve. You will see the humour once I explain. You must seek out the old man of the stone."

"The stone is somewhere near the Men an Tol?" Laurel asked. "He lives near a certain stone?" Her heart sank at the thought. There were countless numbers of stones scattered all over the Hundreds of Penwith. Stone circles and menhirs, not to mention the rocky cliffs towering over the sea.

"Not exactly, he lives within the stone, in a manner of speaking," the Lady replied.

"The stone is used like a portal? Like I used the Men an Tol?" Laurel was confused.

"A portal of sorts, but not the way you are thinking. He is the spirit of the stone and is older than any of us who dwell that half step sideways from the world as you know it."

"How am I supposed to contact him? Will he understand me?"

"Peace, Laurel Rowan. He dwells in the upright stone, the menhir, that you mortals call the Men Scryfa. It should be of little bother for you to find it."

"Men Scryfa? What does that mean? I think *men* means stone but I've never heard the other word."

"In your language it translates from the old Cornish to Literate Stone," the Lady replied.

'The stone talks, then?"

"In truth, it does. But the name comes from the words carved on the face of the stone. If you trace the correct symbols with your finger you will wake the spirit within. Whether he will speak with you or not is his choice."

"What symbols do I need to trace?"

The Lady shook her head. "That is for you to decide when you arrive there. Trust your heart and let it guide your hand." She cocked her head for a moment and the breeze in the upper reaches of the trees grew stronger. "I must go, dear child. I wish you luck on your journey. Go gently." The luminous figure blessed Laurel, resting a hand on her head.

Laurel blinked as a beam of sunlight lanced through the green gloom of the glade. When her vision cleared of the spots dancing before her, the Lady was gone. "I've got to tell Sarie and Gramma about this," she spoke aloud. She stopped at the lip of the first waterfall. "Thank you!" she called. The air caressed her forehead like a kiss.

It seemed to take forever to get out of the valley and across the field to Sarie's house. On her way past the grazing ponies, she stopped by Gort's pony and hugged him. "Thank you," she whispered into his silky neck. Releasing him, she jogged the rest of the way to the fence. Slipping through the fence, Laurel raced down the beaten path to the back door.

"Gramma! Sarie! Wait til I tell you what happened…" She skidded to a halt at the entrance to the kitchen. Sarie stood at the counter with the sun behind her streaming in the windows. Laurel's three friends sat at the table. All of them looked unhappy and worried. "What is it? What's wrong?"

"Where have you been, Laurel?" Sarie demanded. "Bella's gone haring off to Nanjizal without us. I thought she was with you out by the pony field, but my car is missing and so is she. Oh, Bella, what have you done now?" Sarie almost wailed the last words.

Coll's chair crashed to the floor startling Laurel. She whipped toward the sound to see him gripping the edge of the table, his blond hair sticking straight up in front as if he had just thrust his fingers through it. "We can take Emily's car. I dropped her off in Marazion on the way out here. It'll be a tight squeeze but I think we can all fit in. It's bigger than my little mini at any rate." He turned and set the chair upright, pushing it under the table.

"Let's shake a leg, then. The silly woman's got a head start on us." Sarie snatched up her coat and shoved her feet into a pair of boots by the door.

Almost before Laurel could blink, she was in the back of the car with Gort and Aisling. Sarie rode shotgun in front beside Coll. He caught her eye in the rear view mirror and smiled. Laurel's stomach did a queer twisting thing and a thrill of happiness ran through her.

They stopped briefly at Phillip's Pasty Shop in Marazion where Emily was waiting for Coll to pick her up. "Oh my, you've got a full load, I see." Emily waved at Sarie to stay where she was and squeezed into the rear. Gort lifted Aisling up to sit on his lap. Laurel grinned, marvelling at how different he was from the shy stuttering kid he'd been when she first met him.

"What's the occasion?" Emily looked at Laurel.

"Bella's run off to meet Vear Du. Nothing's changed in all the years she's been away, still haring off without thinking things through…and she took my car." Sarie was thoroughly pissed off if the tone of her voice and the pinched look on her face was anything to go by.

Laurel was glad it wasn't herself the woman was annoyed with.

"How is Bella? We haven't had time for a good natter, yet. I was hoping to do that today," Emily said.

“Bella is the same as she ever was. Impatient and impulsive. She’ll be in the middle of a mess before she realizes it—”

“And she’ll expect us to bail her out again,” Emily interrupted her.

“So it would seem.” Sarie snorted and mumbled something under her breath.

“Where are we off to? And Coll, please do slow down.” Emily gripped the back of the front seat for support as the car careened into the roundabout near the Penzance Superstore.

“Gotta drive with the traffic, Grandma,” Coll tossed the words over his shoulder without taking his eyes from the busy traffic.

“How do you know when to go?” The cars seemed to be going way too fast and with no guidance Laurel could see. Some vehicles merged onto the circle without hesitating, others stopped and waited. What they were waiting for was more than Laurel could figure out.

Coll flashed her a wild smile in the rear view mirror. “I just go,” he said.

“Coll!” Emily scolded him. “You just better not get a dent in my car, young man.”

Aisling glanced at Laurel and grinned.

“Do we know where Bella is headed?” Emily tried again to find out their destination.

“Nanjizal,” Sarie clipped the word off and clenched her jaw.

“Mill Bay?” Emily used the alternate name for the little cove. “She’s not planning to meet up with poor old Treagle, is she? He’ll be far too busy moving that sand into the bay to be of any help.” Emily referred to the legend of the demon Treagle, doomed for eternity to sweep the shifting sands from Porthcurnow Cove round Tol-Pedn-Penwith into Nanjizal Bay. The Gulf Stream churning by in the opposite direction ensuring his task was never ending.

A fission of fright curled through Laurel, the last thing she wanted was to confront a demon. Although after Gwin ap Nudd, maybe a mere demon wouldn't be so bad. "She's gone to meet up with Vear Du," Laurel said.

"She can't. The Council forbid him from communicating with mortals, didn't they?" Emily tapped Sarie on the shoulder.

"They did, but…Treagle hates the Council and he's only too happy to run a bit of magical interference to hide the fact they are together." Sarie didn't sound thrilled about the idea.

"I have to tell you what happened in the field, down in the valley," Laurel interrupted. She bounced on the seat in her excitement.

"Leave off, will ya?" Gort protested as Aisling slid a bit on his lap.

"But it's important, I need to tell you," she insisted.

"What is it then?" Sarie glanced over her shoulder.

"I was standing by the fence and Gort's pony made me go with him down into the little gully in the field," she began.

"The Lady's Vale?" Sarie interrupted her.

"Sure, the gully with the stream and the marsh at the bottom. Anyway, I went to the spring and the Lady showed up. I asked her about Gramma and Vear, but she said she couldn't help me."

"Figures," Coll muttered. "They only help if it benefits them."

"That's not true," Laurel objected. "She said she couldn't help me, but that I should go and talk to the old man in the Men Scryfa. The Lady said he might be willing to help us."

"Hmmm, now isn't that interesting?" Emily mused.

"Do you know where the stone thing is? She said it was near the Men an Tol, but that was all." Laurel looked at Aisling.

"I've been there a very long time ago, but we'll need to look at an ordinance survey map to be sure. I think the Nine Maidens Stone Circle is nearby," Sarie said. She rummaged in the glove box.

Not long after the car whipped past the turnoff for the Minack Open-Air Theatre, Coll slowed and parked in a layby just south of Polgigga. He engaged the parking brake and stepped out of the car, shoving the keys in his jeans pocket. Sarie's little car was pulled up on the grassy verge just ahead of them. Once everyone was standing outside, Sarie led the way down a laneway bordered with high hedges of blackberry and raspberry canes. Laurel marvelled at the height and thickness of the plants, growing as they did on top of dry stone walls that were completely concealed from view.

Aisling pointed as a small flock of brightly coloured Red Admiral butterflies rose in a spiral as they passed. Laurel found it strange to walk along what was obviously a private drive and then through the yard of Bosistow Farm. The stone house looked solid and inviting, it blocked a bit of the wind as they walked in the lee of it. It wasn't long before they left the hedgerows behind and followed the beaten path onto the moor. Purple heather and golden gorse carpeted the rolling swell of the land. Laurel inhaled the heady scent of coconut and vanilla as her leg brushed the low growing bushes in passing. Sarie halted and shaded her eyes with her hand.

"I don't see her anywhere. Bella must already be at Nanjizal."

Laurel had to stretch her legs to keep up with Sarie's increased pace. She spared a moment to admire the massive granite rock perched on the edge of Carn Les Boel. *What a perfect way to mark where the Michael and Mary earth energy lines enter England.* There was a node point where the lines crossed each other a short distance from the marker but there was no time to appreciate it now. She jogged to catch up with the others as they followed the South-West Cornish Coastal Path across the broad shoulder of Bosistow Cliff toward the steep path that led down to the cove.

"Oh my," Emily paused to wipe perspiration off her face, "I didn't realize I've been such a slug a bed."

Coll laughed at her and waited for her to catch up to him at the gate partway down the sharp incline. Laurel scanned what she could see of the sandy beach, but Gramma Bella was nowhere to be seen. "Hell and damnation," she muttered. "Why couldn't she have just waited for me?"

"Don't you mean waited for us?"

Laurel squeaked in surprise at the unexpected sound of Aisling's voice close to her ear.

"Sure, waited for us," she agreed.

Sarie reached the bottom of the cliff first and hurried to the wooden set of steps leading down to the beach proper. Laurel reached the bridge over the stream that ran down to join the sea as Sarie jumped the last step down onto the sand.

"Bella! Bella! Wait!"

Laurel raced to the steep steps and almost fell down them in her hurry. Coll was right behind her and caught her about the waist to keep her from pitching into the soft sand. She shook him off and ran to Sarie. The high slit in the rocks shimmered in the sunlight. Gramma Bella was almost to the end of the narrow fissure. The figure of a large man was silhouetted against the brightness at the base of the slit. Her heart leapt in recognition.

"Bella, stop," Sarie called.

Laurel passed her as she ran to reach her grandmother. "Gramma, wait, wait for me," she called breathlessly. The wind whipped the words from her lips and threw them at the towering rock cliffs. *She can't hear me.* "Gramma!" She struggled to move faster over the uneven sand, hard up-thrust ripples left by the receding tide threatened to send her sprawling on her face.

Bella stopped short when she reached the widest spot at the bottom of the slash in the rock. The opening narrowed as it speared upward. Laurel ran harder. Vear Du reached out his hand toward Bella and she clasped it. The air seemed to shimmer and whirl with rainbow colours and shadows. Sarie pulled Laurel up short by the collar of her jacket before she could reach her grandmother. She twisted and fought to free herself.

"Let me go, Sarie! I have to stop her," Laurel pleaded.

Coll stumbled up beside them leaning forward with his hands on his knees to catch his breath.

"Hold onto her, Coll," Sarie commanded as he straightened. "Don't let her come near the portal. Do you understand? No matter what happens. I'm depending on you."

Coll nodded and put both arms around Laurel from behind, holding her against his body. "Let me go." Laurel fought back tears of frustration. Something terrible was going to happen, she just knew it.

With a backward glance to be sure Coll still had Laurel pinioned, she strode forward. "Bella, think about what you're doing. You're only going to make it worse for the selkie." She attempted to get Bella to see reason.

"No, I can help him," she insisted without turning away from the opening.

"Arabella, for God's sake use some common sense for a change. This is madness. What about Laurel? Are you willing to walk away from her?"

"Gramma Bella," Laurel wailed. The realization that her grandmother was planning to go with Vear Du, and maybe never return, hit her like a physical blow. Her knees sagged and she leaned on Coll for support.

Bella half-turned at the sound of her voice. She met Laurel's anguished gaze over Sarie's shoulder. "You don't understand, Laurel. I have to go with him. When you're older you'll see that I am right to do this."

"Time is short, my love. If you're coming, do it now. We need to be moving on. Treagle can only keep the Council's searchers at bay for a short time," Vear Du's deep voice reached Laurel's ears.

"I'm ready," Bella said firmly.

"I'm sorry, little one. But it's not forever if you don't wish it to be. You still have my talisman and it is still potent," Vear spoke directly to Laurel as if her were standing beside her.

Sarie lunged forward and threw herself at Bella while the wind suddenly picked up throwing loose sand and sea spray high into the air.

Through her tears Laurel watched as Bella stepped into the portal without a backward glance. Wild music swelled, vibrating in her breast bone. "No!" The wind caught her words and threw them back at her.

Coll fell to his knees, taking Laurel with him. Sarie lay sprawled on the wet sand by the portal. Laurel blinked the sand from her eyes. The split in the rock stood empty. No sign of Gramma Bella or Vear Du. Sobs shook her and she welcomed the solid comfort of Coll's arms around her.

"Did you see that?" Gort's voice was incredulous. "They just disappeared, just like that." He snapped his fingers.

"Did you hear the music?" Aisling's voice sounded dreamy. "Did you hear it? How beautiful it was." She took a step toward the rock split. "I want to hear it again,"

"Ash, snap out of it," Gort said giving her a shake. "Stay away from that place."

"Oh, all right. But it was so beautiful…" her voice trailed off.

Gwin Scawen stepped into view beside her, materializing out of thin air. "I'm late, oh dear, I'm too late." The twig thin piskie wrung his hands and hopped from foot to foot. "Oh dear, oh dear. The big 'uns are going to be *gorbolleck*, so they are. So very, very angry they'll be. No telling what they'll do now."

Aisling dropped to her knees beside the distraught little man and attempted to sooth him, her fascination with the music forgotten for the moment.

Laurel struggled to her feet and pulled free of Coll's arms. Trembling, she moved toward the last place she saw Gramma Bella. She reached the rock split and looked down. No foot prints marred the sand. Holding her breath she stuck her hand and arm through the opening before Coll could stop her. Nothing. *She's gone, she's really gone.* "What is this place?" She whirled toward Sarie. "You knew this could happen, didn't you? That's why you were so worried, isn't it?"

"No, Laurel. I had no idea the place had so much power. They call it Zawn Pys, the Song of the Sea. I had no idea it could be used as a portal. I just know what Bella is like when she gets the bit in her teeth…" Her voice faltered and tears pooled in her eyes.

Laurel walked all the way through the opening and back again. "Gramma Bella," she screeched, setting the seagulls wheeling overhead to screaming in response. Laurel sank onto the wet sand and put her head in her hands. "Oh, Gramma, why didn't you take me with you?"

Chapter Twelve

Laurel slept late the next morning. When she finally made her way downstairs she found Sarie still sitting at the table, a mug of cold tea in front of her, the milk curdled on top.

"I can't believe she's gone," Sarie spoke slowly as if each word was a chore.

"I know. But she'll come back. Won't she?" Laurel sat down opposite the older woman and clasped her hands together on the linoleum table cover.

"I don't rightly know, Laurel. I just don't know."

Fear and disbelief gathered in her chest. Sarie was never without an answer to even the trickiest of problems. Laurel had never seen her so defeated and without a plan.

"What are we going to do? We have to go after her and bring her back." She drummed her fingers on the table, waiting for Sarie to reply.

After a long time she looked up and met Laurel's gaze. "I don't think she wants to come back."

The words hit Laurel like a physical blow. Shock squeezed the breath from her lungs and her pulse thundered in her ears. "What?" she managed to squeak out.

Without speaking Sarie pulled a crumpled piece of paper out of her shirt pocket and handed it to her. The letter crackled as Laurel took it in her trembling hands and smoothed it out on the table. It was Gramma Bella's dark slanted writing that looked back at her. She had to read it twice before the meaning sank in.

Dearest Sarie,

I hate to leave like this but secrecy is of the utmost importance. I can't risk speaking about my plans as the

Council has spies everywhere. I know you understand a bit of how the other worlds overlap ours and that they exist side by side. So you will see what I am proposing is possible. I have spoken with Vear and he told me that he would gladly have accepted his exile if I hadn't come back to Cornwall. But now that I am here we cannot stand to be apart. I am to meet him at the portal in Nanjizal, (did you ever guess that split in the rocks was a doorway to the barrow world and others? I never did), then we'll disappear into the other worlds. Vear says they are like unpeeling an onion, layers upon layers of worlds. Some very much like the one we know and others that are vastly different. The plan (which you must never speak aloud) is to slip from layer to layer and avoid anyone the Council might send after us.

I hate to leave Laurel so soon after I have just reconnected with her again, but all I can think of is being with Vear again. He doesn't mind that I am not the young woman I was when he last saw me. He hasn't aged very much at all and so we make an odd couple, but inside my heart where it counts I am still that young girl who fell in love with him all those years ago. Please try to explain all this to Laurel and tell her how much I love her.

Don't try to come after me and don't let Laurel and her friends try to find me. It would be dangerous for everyone involved. I am happier than I have been since I left Vear Du's cave, it seems so long ago now. I could weep for all the wasted years. I would write more but time is short and it is time I was going. I apologize for taking your car. You will find it in the layby near Polgigga, the keys under the driver side floor mat. (I know that's not very original, but there it is). Please don't follow me or try to stop me. You've always said I was impetuous and impulsive, but I've thought this through, I really have.

Love always, Bella oxoxox

The note slipped through Laurel's fingers and she blinked back tears. "How can she just leave me like this? There's so much I want to say to her and I wanted to get to know her better…" her voice trailed off and she blew her nose on the sleeve of her flannel shirt.

"Laurel! Here use this." Sarie handed her a tissue.

"Thanks," she muttered.

"To answer your question, I've known Bella since we were kids and much as I love her and it pains me to say this, Bella's wants and needs have always come first with her. Never doubt that she loves you very much, but she loves herself better than anyone. When Bella set her mind to something she wouldn't rest til she got it." Sarie sighed and looked down at the cold tea in front of her.

"But knowing what you want and going after it is good, isn't it?" Laurel asked.

"I suppose it is. But only if the pursuit of what a person desires doesn't hurt others in the process." Sarie held Laurel's gaze.

"Like now?" Laurel guessed.

"Yes, like now. Bella is so blinded by her need to be with Vear she has forgotten how many years have passed and that she is no longer a young girl. She has given little thought to how this will affect you," she held up her hand when Laurel would have interrupted her, "and she has not taken into account how her actions will reflect on her friends in the other worlds. Vear Du himself, Gwin Scawen, Belerion, Morgawr…they will all be suspected of aiding and abetting her. Depending on the mood of the Council there might be severe penalty meted out."

"Do you think we should go and find that standing stone the Lady told me about?" Laurel looked at Sarie hopefully.

"The Men Scryfa? I've never met the old man in the stone, but if the Lady thinks he might have a solution for Bella and Vear then perhaps the best thing would be to speak with him as soon as possible." She reached across the table and squeezed Laurel's hand. "Maybe together we can talk some sense into your grandmother. If we can find her."

"I'll call Coll and get him to bring Gort and Ash with him. Once we're all together we can figure out a plan." Laurel jumped up and went to make the call.

* * *

"Your grandmother sure has a one track mind, doesn't she?" Gort handed Bella's letter to Coll. Aisling having read it at the same time as Gort.

"So it would seem," Laurel agreed. "I wish she'd talked to me about it before she took off."

"Or me," Sarie said.

"You said you wanted us all here to decide what to do, so do you have a plan?" Coll finished reading the letter and gave it back to Sarie.

"I think we need to go and find that standing stone the Lady told me about," Laurel replied.

"The one near the Men an Tol?" Gort asked.

Laurel nodded. "Do you guys know how to find it?"

"I can ask Gwin if he'll take us to it," Aisling offered.

"That's brill, so it is." Gort smiled at her.

"Back in a minute." Ash left the table and went out to the garden.

Sarie got up and left the kitchen, returning a few minutes later with a folded map. Laurel moved the mugs while Sarie spread the ordinance survey map out on the table. "The Men an Tol is here." She pointed to the location of the holed stone. "Which way is the Men Scryfa from there, do you three have any idea?"

Laurel looked hopefully at her friends. Disappointment threatened to overwhelm her when they shook their heads. Pushing the emotion away, she leaned forward to see the small print on the map better.

"There! It says 'standing stone', just to the northeast of the Men an Tol." Coll pointed to the map. "It's right near the Nine Maidens Stone Circle."

Sarie shook her head. "I don't think that's it. It should be identified by name if I remember right."

"Here it is, look if we follow the track past the style where the path goes off toward the Men an Tol and keep going to where it turns toward the coast we can double back on the path to the southwest. It should take us there." Gort traced the route with a finger.

The back door opened to admit Aisling. She leaned over Gort's shoulder to see what he was pointing to. "Oh, good. You've found it on the map at least. I can't get Gwin to talk to me. It's like he's just disappeared." A frown wrinkled her forehead. "He's never failed to show up when I called before. You don't think he's in trouble because of what happened at Nanjizal, do you? Him and the selkie are really close, he might be helping them hide."

"That's likely, I'm afraid." Sarie scrubbed her hands over her face. "Their friendship goes way back to long before Bella and I ever met them."

"How did you get to know them? Was it a long time ago?" Laurel asked.

"It's a long story, too complicated to go into right now. We were both pretty young when we came across them for the first time. Bella met Vear first when she was out riding. She didn't know who or what he was at the time, though. Later, she met Gwin when Vear came to her rescue out in Lamorna Cove. She was hiding out from her father because he wanted her to marry Daniel Treliving—"

"My Uncle Daniel, how could her da think that was a good idea?" Gort interrupted her.

"Heaven only knows, Daniel was a bounder and he wasn't any nicer as a young man than he was when you knew him. Brian, your father, was so unlike him it was hard to believe they were brothers." Sarie continued. "That's all we have time for right now. We should get a move on and see if we can convince the Men Scryfa to communicate with us."

"I'll call Gramma and let her know what we're up to. She says she's going to her workroom to support us from there," Coll said.

"That's good, we can use all the help we can get right now," Sarie replied.

"I wonder where Gwin is, it's not like him to just disappear," Aisling worried.

"Maybe he'll show up at the stone," Coll suggested. "Remember how he showed up at the Men an Tol that time in the storm?"

"Maybe, I hope you're right." Aisling didn't sound convinced.

"Okay, you lot. Let's get a move on. We'll take Emily's car as it has a bit more room than mine. I'll drive." Sarie held out her hand for the keys which Coll reluctantly handed over.

Laurel was last out the door and secured it behind them. She got into the passenger seat as the others were already in the rear seat. Sarie let out the clutch as soon as the door was shut and they bumped down the lane to the road. Sarie joined the A30 just past Chyandour, skirted Penzance and at the roundabout at Heamoor took the 132 toward Madron. Laurel glanced at the sign indicating the entrance to Madron Holy Well, wishing they had time to go and visit it. A short time later they passed the Lanyon Tea House and she could pick out the Men an Tol amidst the heather and gorse on the rising land just to the northwest.

There were no cars in the layby at the foot of the track to the Men an Tol. The sun was warm for December, but the wind had a knife edge to it. Laurel was glad of the high collar on her coat. Without waiting for the others to join her, she set off up the rutted track. She turned her head and smiled at Coll as he caught up to her and took her hand. Before they reached the style on the right hand side that led to the Men an Tol, Sarie, Gort, and Aisling were right behind them.

"Do you think we should take the time to detour to the Men an Tol and see if I can reach Gwin from there?" Aisling slowed as they passed the entrance.

"You go if you want, Ash. I want to find the Men Scryfa as quick as possible." Laurel didn't alter her pace.

"If he was anywhere around he'd just show up," Gort said.

"I suppose you're right," Ash agreed reluctantly.

By the time they reached the spot where the track turned to the west, Laurel's ears were ringing from the wind whipping over the moor. She stopped and looked for the path that should angle back the way they had come, running roughly parallel to the more travelled track they just walked. There was nothing clearly marking the way and she waited impatiently for Sarie. Using Coll's tall figure for a windbreak, Sarie consulted the ordinance survey map.

"It should be that way." She pointed to the right as she faced the way they had just come.

Laurel set off ahead of the others who trailed behind her. She topped the sloping rise of the land and came to a break in the hedge surrounding an open field.

"There it is!" She pointed toward the middle of the rolling field where a single stone thrust up against the sky. Breaking into a jog, she set off across the short wind-tossed grass. She was surprised to find the menhir was taller than her when she reached it. The writing carved into the north face was over grown with lichen but was still quite visible. "What does it say?" Laurel tilted her head to one side as she tried to make sense of the symbols.

"It's written in Latin", Sarie said. "*Rialobrani Cunovali fili.* It means Rialobrani the son of Cunovalus. Rialobran might mean 'royal raven' in old Cornish."

"Is some guy buried here?" Coll took a step back away from the stone.

"No one is sure if that's true or not. There's a legend about there being a battle nearby and that the king was killed and buried here. The stone is supposed to be the same height as the warrior."

"Well, let's just hope whoever the Lady was talking about is in there and willing to talk to us," Gort said.

"Do you have any idea how we're supposed to contact him?" Laurel looked dubiously at the tall stone and then at Sarie.

"I think," she paused for a moment, "since the White Lady spoke to you about it, you should be the one to attempt it. Try putting your hand on the stone and closing your eyes. See if you can hear or see anything that way," Sarie suggested.

“Okay, I guess.” Laurel glanced at Coll.

His face was white and drawn, but he nodded his agreement with Sarie’s words. Laurel reached out and grasped his hand before she placed her left hand tentatively on the rough surface of the granite. Taking a deep breath she closed her eyes and reached out to the stone with her thoughts. Her fingers traced the rough lichen covered surface, bumping over the carved letters. The wind sweeping across the moor seemed louder with her eyes shut. Laurel imagined she heard the sea booming on the sea cliffs far to the west. For the longest time nothing felt any different and her thoughts began to wander. Without warning the stone beneath her hand became warm and then hot.

“Bloody hell!” Coll pulled Laurel away from the stone and she rounded on him ready to rip a strip off him.

“Why’d you do that?” she yelled. “Something was finally happening.” She looked past him at Gort and Aisling. Both her friends were looking past her with stunned expressions on their faces. She glanced back at Coll. His face was paper white and his eyes wide and staring.

“Turn around, Laurel,” Sarie said calmly, although her face was pale as well.

Laurel pivoted about and gasped. Standing in front of the tall hoary menhir was a very old man. She took an involuntary step backward and bumped into Coll who put his arms around her waist. His presence helped chase the shock away and loosen her tongue.

“Hello,” she stuttered. “I’m Laurel and these are my friends.” She waved vaguely behind her.

The figure shook itself, dust and moss falling from the folds of his voluminous cloak. The hood fell back to reveal long gray hair falling over his shoulders like threads of shining silk. The craggy face split into a grin, the steel gray eyes sparkling with amusement.

“Well met, young miss.” The voice was gravelly, but not unkind. “It has been many long years since a mortal has called me from my stone.” His gaze travelled over the huddle of Laurel and her friends. "It seems much has changed since I last walked this earth if your raiment is any indication."

"My what?" Laurel was startled into asking.

"Raiment, what you are wearing," he explained.

"Oh." She blushed and glanced down at her jeans and shirt.

"But I digress, that is of little importance. Why, pray chance, did you summon me hence?"

Laurel swallowed and glanced at Gort and Aisling. They were ranged with Sarie a bit behind and to the sides of where she stood. From the astounded expressions on their faces, Laurel figured they weren't interested in taking part in the conversation. Coll tightened his hold a little and bent to whisper in her ear.

"You called him, so go ahead and ask his assistance."

"Um, I'm sorry to disturb you…" she began.

"You're not disturbing me, dear heart. I welcome the chance to feel the sun on my face again. Now go on, what is it you called me for?"

"Um, okay then…my grandmother is friends with a selkie. His name is Vear Du and she met him a long time ago when she was pretty young—"

He held up a hand to stop her. "Ah, yes. The mortal and the selkie. Even I, in my stone, have heard the ripples and disturbances caused in the worlds by their situation. But what has that to do with you, young lady?"

"Well, the mortal," Laurel stumbled over the word, "is my gramma. She loves Vear Du, she really truly does. I asked the White Lady of the spring in Sarie's field," she gestured toward Sarie as she spoke. "I asked her if she knew of a way for them to be together without everyone, including the Council, getting all bent out of shape over it."

A grin crossed the rugged face and his shoulders shook with laughter. "All bent out of shape, what an amusing thought. Go on, dear, go on."

"Well, she said there was nothing she could do, but suggested that I seek the Men Scryfa and ask your advice. So, is there a way, is it possible for Gramma Bella and Vear

Du to be together, even for a short time?" Laurel leaned back against Coll for support. Her ears were ringing and the world seemed tilted sideways.

"Peace, child. Let me think on this for a moment." He folded his hands inside the long sleeves of his rusty coloured cloak and closed his eyes.

Laurel hardly dared to breathe for fear of disturbing his concentration. If this lead didn't pan out she had nowhere else to turn.

Finally, he opened his eyes and studied her. She wanted to squirm under the scrutiny but forced herself to stay still and return his stare. He nodded, as if coming to some conclusion.

"There may be a way. But it is not without risk. Are you prepared to accept whatever consequences may result from your endeavours?"

"I am." Laurel nodded. "If I can see Gramma Bella again, and if she can be happy with Vear Du, I'm willing."

"And you?" The old man looked over her head at Coll.

"I go where she goes," he said. Laurel thought his voice sounded kind of strangled.

"I fear I don't need to inquire of you, friend of Gwin Scawen and the small folk, or you, *anam cara* of the crystal stallion. But, good manners insist that I ask anyway."

"We are willing," Gort and Aisling spoke together and grinned at each other.

"You," he tipped his head toward Sarie, "you, I will need to hold space for the travellers so they will be able to find the portal and return to this world when the time comes. Are you willing?"

"Aye, of course, I am," Sarie replied.

"Fine then." He rummaged under his cloak in the folds of his robe. He detached a leather pouch from his belt and upended it over his large palm. Laurel leaned forward to see what he held.

"These are tokens that will allow you to enter the other worlds. They will also shield you from notice by the Council and its creatures. You must keep them on your person at all times. Woe betide you if you lose them, for without them there will be no way to return to your world, and I will not be able to search you out and assist in any way. Do you understand?"

Laurel nodded, not trusting her voice not to break. The others must have done the same because the old man smiled at her.

"Come then and collect what is yours," he beckoned them.

Laurel approached first and held out her hand.

"This is yours, Laurel Rowan." He handed her a smooth round stone disc with a strange symbol etched on it.

"What does it mean, and how do you know my name?" she asked.

"All the worlds know your name and that of your companions. It is not every daughter of Eve who can bargain with Gwin ap Nudd and win." A dry chuckle emerged from behind the tangled beard. "I will explain about the symbols once each has claimed their own."

Coll stepped forward and accepted his stone. The old man placed a horny hand on his head as he took the talisman. "Blessings on you, the protector."

Aisling went next. She looked up at the man with shining eyes. "I never thought to meet a stone man in my wildest dreams," she whispered. He blessed her as well.

Gort stepped forward, took his disc and bowed his head in thanks. The man laid both hands on the boy's shoulders and offered his blessings.

To Sarie, he smiled and motioned her forward. He pressed something into her hand that Laurel couldn't see. Sarie glanced down at it and smiled before tucking it in her pocket. "Thank you," she whispered.

"Now, gather round and I will explain what the symbols represent. The marks on the stones are from the ancient ogham alphabet. It is one of the first forms of writing that existed, but it has been mostly lost through long years of disuse."

"What is it, and how do you read it?" Laurel turned the smooth stone over and over in her hand.

"It is really quite simple if you know the trick. You start with a straight staff and the alphabet is divided into five divisions. The first group is BLFSN, the second is HDTCQ, thc third is M,G,Ng,Ss,R, the fourth is AOUEI, and the fifth is what is known as the dipthongs, CH,TH,PR,PH and XI."

"Are we supposed to remember all that?" Coll exclaimed.

"No, young sir. Not at all. I just want you to have some understanding of the marks. Now each letter is also associated with a tree, and each carries a hidden meaning. Now to write these marks, which only those who have studied the oghams will understand, you start, as I have said, with a straight staff. The first group of letters have dashes on the right side of the staff. B for Beith or Birch, is one dash, L for Luis or Rowan, is two dashes, F for Fearn or Alder, is three dashes, S for Saille or Willow has four dashes and N for Nuin or Ash has five straight dashes. The next five are the same except the dashes are on the left side of the straight staff. The group that begins with M for Muin or Vine, is similar except the dashes are on an angle across the straight staff, with the highest part of the dash on the left of the staff. The next group has the dashes straight across the staff at right angles to it. The last group which is the dipthongs are different. Although they are set on the straight staff as well, they have symbols rather than dashes. CH for Koad or Grove is an X centered on the staff, TH for Oir or Spindle Tree is a diamond centered on the staff, PE for Uilleand or Honeysuckle is a double X situated on the right side of the staff overlapping each other, PH for Phagos or Beech resembles the hook of a shepherd's crook and is on the right side of the staff, lastly is XI for Mor or the Sea, this is a box divided into nine equal parts and situated on the right side of straight staff."

"That's not making it much clearer," Coll grumbled. Laurel kicked him in the shin to silence him.

The old man grinned. "You need only concern yourselves with the ogham I have given you. Coll, yours, if you will look please, is four dashes on the left of the staff which is Hazel or Coll. Aisling, yours is five dashes on the right of the staff which is Nuin or Ash. Gort, yours is two dashes at an angle across the central staff which is Ivy or Gort. Laurel, yours is, as you may have guessed by now, two dashes on the right of the staff representing Luis or Rowan. These will guard and protect you in the other worlds and should you become separated or lost will guide you to safety.

"Now, Sarie. Yours is most different of all. You are the gate keeper where you will hold sacred space for the journeyers. Your stone represents the Crane Bag and holds the five letters of the last group. On it are the X which represents shears, the diamond represents a helmet, the double X represent bones, the hook represents itself, the nine times divided box represents the house which holds them. Each has a use and purpose which you will discover should you have need of it. With these talismans you can journey as safely as any mortal can into the other worlds."

"Thank you." Sarie bowed her head.

"Thank you," Laurel chorused in time with her friends.

The old man of the stone raised his hand palm turned out toward them and intoned a blessing in a language that flowed like music in Laurel's ear. When the ringing tones had died away, he shook himself and straightened the folds of his cloak about him. "I have stayed too long in the world of man. It wearies me with its constant movement and the reek of iron overshadows the sweet scent of the tin of Kernow. I take my leave of you now, daughter of Eve." He placed a hand on Laurel's shoulder for a moment before he turned toward the tall standing stone at his back.

"Wait, can I ask your name?" Laurel reached out to grasp the folds of his cloak.

He turned back toward her. "True names have power, but you may call me Rialobran."

"Thank you, Rialobran," she said.

He tipped his hoary head in acknowledgement. The harsh cry of a pair of ravens diving across the sky not two feet above her head made her duck and glance upward. She looked back to the stone in time to see the last bit of the old man's foot and the tip of his hood fade back into the lichen covered stone. When she reached out and laid her hand on it, the granite was warm even though the wind sweeping across the open field was cold and damp with the promise of rain.

"Did you see that? Did any of you see him leave?" Laurel spun around toward her friends.

Gort and Coll shook their heads. Aisling smiled and shook her head as well. "The ravens distracted us," Sarie said. "Just as he planned it, I'm sure."

"Let's get back to the car before the rain starts." Coll turned the collar of his coat up and started back across the ankle deep grass. Aisling and Gort followed. Laurel smiled to see them holding hands.

"C'mon, girl. The weather doesn't wait for anyone. If we don't reach the car in time we'll be soaked to the skin." Sarie touched her arm.

"It was real, wasn't it? I didn't just dream that an old man came out of the stone?" Laurel felt light headed as if she just got off one of those amusement park rides that spun you around. She was reluctant to remove her hand from the menhir.

"Yes, it was very real. You're holding the proof of it in your hand," Sarie said, opening her hand to display the stone disc resting on her palm.

"Let's get a move on. The last thing we need is for one of you to catch your death of cold out here." Sarie moved onto the muddy path and waited for Laurel to join her.

"Go gently," Laurel whispered and let her fingers caress the rough stone. "Coming, Sarie."

The wind whipped the hair over her face and buffeted her back, lending impetuous to her steps. Overhead, four ravens wove patterns against the gunmetal sky, the bellies of the clouds swollen with rain.

Chapter Thirteen

The rain beat on the kitchen windows, beads of water gleaming black against the panes. A rush of cold air announced Sarie's return from putting the ponies up for the night. Laurel got to her feet and poured hot tea into a fresh mug and set it by Sarie's place at the table.

"It's a wild night out there," the older woman remarked. Moisture sparkled in her silver hair as she passed under the overhead light.

"I'm glad we were home before the storm hit proper. It would have been hell to get caught in this out in the open." Coll wrapped his hands around the mug of tea.

"I'll ring Emily and let her know the outcome of our little adventure this afternoon. If she's agreeable to being alone tonight, I'd rather you boys stay here for the night. The tide's high and there'll be a storm surge with this blow, the waves might well be up over the motorway between Marazion and Penzance," Sarie said. "You'd best phone your mum too, Aisling."

Aisling made a face as she lifted the receiver and placed the call. "You know she's going to have kittens about me not being home and a storm raging. It's not like I'm out on the Wherry Rocks or anything." She heaved a sigh as the call rang through. Twenty minutes later she broke the connection and handed the phone to Sarie. "Mum's not happy, but I told her Sarie wouldn't let the boys drive in this weather and I had no other way to get home. She tried to badger Dad into coming to collect me, but he said I was fine where I was. So, you're stuck with me." She grinned and sat next to Gort.

Sarie took the mobile and went out into the hall to ring Emily. Coll's gaze followed her exit, a worried frown creasing his forehead. “I wonder what’s so secret we can’t hear about it?” he grumbled.

Laurel put her hand over his and squeezed. “She probably wants to know how whatever Emily was doing in her workroom to support us today turned out. I haven’t a clue what she was doing, do you?”

“Nah, Emily keeps that room locked. She’d skin me if I even peeked in the keyhole,” Coll answered.

“She’ll want to tell her about the stone discs for sure. Maybe ask her advice about all that holding space stuff the stone man talked about. Any notion how someone would go about that?” Gort looked at Aisling.

“Have you heard from Gwin?” Laurel suddenly remembered the piskie and his unexpected absence.

Ash shook her head. “I’m really starting to get worried. He’s never been away this long before.”

Laurel pulled her stone disc from the pocket of her jeans. The talisman Vear Du gave come out with it, the thong tangled about the green serpentine disc. She held it in her fingers for a moment after pulling the stone free. “I wonder if I can find Gramma Bella and him using this?” She held it up so the cowrie shell twirled in the light.

“It might be dangerous for them, Laurel,” Ash cautioned her. “Better wait and ask Sarie when she’s finished on the phone.”

“You’re probably right, as usual. It’s just so tempting.” She ran the leather thong through her fingers and placed it on the table next the disc.

“There, everything is set to rights,” Sarie sounded pleased with herself. She came and joined them.

“Do you think Gwin is with Gramma and Vear?” Laurel asked.

“You still can’t reach him?” She looked at Aisling who shook her head. “Well, then it is very likely that’s where he is.”

“I still have the talisman Vear gave me, should I try to find them with it?” Laurel picked it up and held it to the light.

A violent gust of wind hit the house, rattling the windows in their frame. She jumped and almost dropped the charm. She whipped around and stared at the low bank of windows. A dark green face seemed to be pressed against the pane of the one farthest from her, long snakes of tangled hair waving about the head. When she blinked the image was gone. Shivering, she turned back to the table and leaned on Coll for comfort.

"That may, or may not, have been a sign of disapproval." Sarie eyed Laurel. "What did you see that has your face pale as milk?

"Nothing, it was just the rain hitting the window." She shivered again and tucked the charm in her pocket.

"I thought I saw Treagle," Gort whispered. "All green faced and buggy eyes…"

"It's just the storm." Aisling pushed a lock of hair off his forehead.

Sarie pushed back from the table and carried her mug to the sink. "It's getting late, time we were all in bed."

Laurel got up and took her mug and Coll's to the sink. She ran some water and set about washing up. Aisling joined her and took up a linen towel to dry the clean dishes after depositing the last two mugs into the wash water. Sarie stood by the hall door waiting to extinguish the kitchen light.

"You girls are in Laurel's room, Coll and Gort can share the spare room across the hall since Bella has no need of it right now. I'll clear her things out in the morning. No monkey business, straight to bed and to sleep with you. It's been a long day and who knows what tomorrow may bring." She switched off the overhead light and closed the kitchen door after the girls passed by. Laurel led the way up the dark stairway, the only light coming from the hall light at the top of the landing. The door to the spare room was already closed when she reached the top. Aisling was close on her heels as she pushed open her bedroom door.

"Night, Sarie. We'll do the horses in the morning," Laurel called.

"Night, Sarie," Ash echoed.

“Good night, girls. If you’re up first, by all means please take care of the ponies.” Sarie’s door snicked shut on the last of her words.

“Man, I’m bushed,” Laurel exclaimed, pulling on her pyjamas.

Ash giggled. “I take it that means you’re tired?”

Laurel nodded and slid into the side of the bed closest the wall. The sheets were cold and she hoped they’d warm up quickly. Ash joined her and shoved the pillow up against the headboard so she could sit with her knees drawn up, resting her chin on her forearms.

“I don’t think you should try to use that talisman until we’re through into the other worlds. Even then, what if it brings the Council or their version of the police down on us? It’s too risky. I really wish I could talk to Gwin Scawen. He has to know more about how the politics works than we do,” Aisling said.

“I know,” Laurel agreed. “Did you see that face at the window like Gort and I did? It looked like some drowned sea witch or something.” Laurel shuddered and burrowed deeper under the covers.

The other girl shook her head. “I didn’t notice anything, but Gort’s face went white for a second and he muttered something about Treagle, so maybe he did. We can ask the boys in the morning.”

Laurel closed her eyes and pulled the quilt up over her head. The bed creaked as Aisling stretched out beside her. Willing away the spectre of Treagle, or whatever it was she saw in the window earlier, she forced herself to think about finding the fugitives in some nebulous other worlds. The warmth of the bed and the patter of rain dripping on the wide sill outside the window lulled her into a half-asleep dreamlike state.

The floor boards squeaked and the hinges of the bedroom door creaked. Laurel’s eyes flew open and her heart leaped into her throat. Under the covers Aisling’s hand gripped hers.

“What is it?” Laurel whispered, her voice hoarse with fear.

Ash held a forefinger to her lips, eyes wide and staring in her pale face.

Neither girl wanted to turn and look toward the door. Laurel jumped at the sound of something shuffling across the threshold, the old boards of the floor squeaking as the intruder moved into the room. She was shaking so hard the rustling of the bed clothes sounded loud to her ears. The noise stopped and Laurel dared to turn her head and peek toward the door. A huge hulking shadow towered over the bed. A scream rose in her throat but emerged from her lips as a breathless yelp. The figure loomed larger in the darkness before doubling over.

"Bloody hell," the words hissed into the dark. "Quit shovin'."

"Coll?" Laurel sat bolt upright and reached for the light.

"Don't turn on the light. Sarie'll be onto to us in a flash." It was Gort's voice. The huge shadowy figure resolved itself into two smaller shapes.

"What are you doing scaring the liver out of us?" Ash demanded, sitting up leaning against the headboard.

Laurel squirmed about until she was sitting shoulder to shoulder with her friend. The bed sank and the springs creaked softly as Coll and Gort settled on the end of the bed. "What are you doing in here? It better be good, you scared the bejeesus out of me." She clamped her still shaking hands around her knees and glared at the pair on the end of the bed.

"We need to talk, figure out a plan. I couldn't sleep and neither could Coll, so we snuck over here," Gort explained.

"Uh huh," Laurel grunted. "Did you have to sneak up on us like some weird stalker dude? You couldn't have just whispered 'Hey girls' or something?"

"We didn't want to wake up Sarie," Coll offered. "We didn't think you guys would be asleep yet."

"What is so important it couldn't wait til morning?" Aisling steered the conversation away from what was rapidly developing into an argument between Coll and Laurel.

“I saw Traegle in the kitchen window,” Gort said in a rush, his eyes gleaming in the faint light from the open door.

“I did too,” Laurel whispered. “He had his face smooshed up against the window and his hair was waving around like a bunch of snakes.” She shuddered and pulled the quilt up to her chin.

Gort nodded vehemently and turned to Coll. “See? I told you I did too see him!”

“Hush,” Ash cautioned. “Coll, go shut the door, will you?”

“What do you think it means? The thing peering in the window?” Laurel asked.

Coll shut the door and climbed back on the end of the bed. “Don’t know. Maybe he was spying for the Council.”

“No, Gramma Bella said Treagle was helping Vear Du. More likely he had a message for us from them,” Laurel said. She got up on her knees and peered out the window. “Do you think he’s still out there somewhere?”

“He’s long gone by now. With this wind blowing he’ll be compelled to move the sand around the headland at Nanjizal,” Aisling said. “Sit back down, Laurel. I’m getting cold.”

Laurel slid back under the covers and propped her chin on her knees. “So what’s the plan you were talking about?”

“Don’t have one yet. That’s why we gotta talk to you guys,” Coll muttered.

“I think we should start at Nanjizal, that’s where your gramma went through the portal,” Gort said.

“It’s as good a place as any, I guess. The Men an Tol worked for me last time, but I don’t think it will work this time,” Laurel mused.

“Okay, so we go out to Nanjizal tomorrow. Do we take Sarie and my gramma with us, or sneak off on our own?” Coll strategized.

“The man in the stone said Sarie needed to ‘hold space’ for us, so we have to tell her what we’re doing,” Aisling reminded them.

‘You’re right, I forgot about that,” Coll agreed.

"What do we do at the portal? How does it work?" Gort chewed his bottom lip.

Laurel glanced at Aisling who shrugged helplessly. "Darn that piskie. If he was here I'm sure he could tell us," she whispered fiercely.

"Have you all got those stone discs on you? Mine has a hole in the top, see?" Laurel pulled the disc out from her pyjama top. She'd strung it on a blue ribbon so it hung around her neck.

Aisling picked hers up from the night table and peered at it in the dim light. "It does have a hole! I could swear it wasn't there earlier."

"Hang on, I'll go get ours." Coll slipped off the bed and padded to the door. After checking to be sure the coast was clear he disappeared and reappeared a few minutes later with the discs. He handed Gort's to him and after settling on the bed examined his.

"Here." Laurel pulled some hair ribbons out of the night table drawer. "String them on these, there's less chance of losing them if we wear them."

Aisling yawned. "Okay, so we're going out to the portal in the morning, after we tell Sarie and Emily what we're up to. Yes?"

"But what are we supposed to do when we get there?" Laurel fretted.

"We need to trust that once we're there we'll figure it out," Gort didn't sound convinced.

"The tide has to be out or we can't reach the rock. I can't remember when low tide is tomorrow," Aisling cautioned.

"Sarie has a tide table downstairs. We can check it over breakfast," Laurel said.

"This is getting complicated. Maybe we're on the wrong track," Coll worried.

"We can't settle anything tonight other than we've decided to start at the Nanjizal portal when the tide is out tomorrow. Let's get some sleep and see if things are clearer in the morning," Aisling advised.

Gort and Coll slid off the bed and padded to the door. “Night, Laurel. Night, Ash,” Coll whispered. Gort waved a hand in their direction and peeked out the door. Giving the all clear, he and Coll disappeared and the door snicked shut behind them.

“Do you think we’re doing the right thing?” Laurel slid down into the bed.

“I hope so. At least it’s a start.” Aisling snuggled under the quilt and yawned. “Night.”

“Night,” Laurel echoed. Hard as she tried to sleep, images of Gramma Bella and Vear Du played in a loop through her brain. When she finally fell into a fitful slumber her dreams were plagued by the disembodied head of Treagle, his lips moving frantically. He was replaced by Gramma and Vear running from hiding place to hiding place. Somewhere there was an important message she needed to find, but the harder she looked the more elusive it became. Disjointed words lost in the roar of the wind and the hiss of the sea.

Chapter Fourteen

Morning dawned bright, clear, and frosty. Laurel pulled on a flannel shirt over her t-shirt and jeans. She glanced at the closed door to the spare room before following Aisling down the stairs. Sarie was in the kitchen, the kettle already boiling for the tea.

"Sit you down, girls. Toast will up 'derctly." Sarie waved hand toward the table.

"Boys not up yet?" Laurel asked.

"Haven't heard a peep out of them."

"We need to talk to you, Sarie. But we should wait for the boys," Laurel said.

"Have you come up with a plan, then?" The older woman raised an inquisitive eyebrow.

"I think so," she answered.

"Hey, did you save any for us?" Coll burst through the door followed closely by Gort.

"We did, not that you deserve it, you slug a beds," Aisling countered.

"It were a late night, so it were." Gort yawned and covered his mouth.

The boys pulled out chairs and settled at the table. Sarie set a plate of toast and a pot of preserves on the table, followed by a bowl of boiled eggs. Laurel got up and brought the tea pot over, covering it with a bright knitted cozy to keep it warm while it steeped.

"Eat up, then. You can tell me your plans when you're done. Things always look better on a full stomach." Sarie took her place at the table.

Laurel pushed away the empty mug and looked around the table. Everyone except Coll was finished eating. He was still polishing off the last bit of toast.

"Ash, can you check the tide chart, please?" Laurel began.

She went to fetch the chart while Laurel explained their plan to Sarie.

"Since Gramma used the rock portal at Nanjizal, we figured that's as good a place as any to start. I have no idea how to use the thing, or activate it, or whatever it is we need to do to it. The man in the stone said we needed you to 'hold space' for us. Does that mean you have to be out at the bay, or somewhere else to do that? Coll thought Emily might be able to help you with that, if you think it would be okay."

"If you can get the portal to work, how will you know where to go? Remember, the other worlds are like an onion, each world layered on top of the next. Time runs differently in those places, some will be slower, and some much faster. It is very hard to judge the passage of time, what might seem like only a few minutes may be days or years in this world. Or what you think are weeks or months passing might only be minutes here. What is your plan to find Bella?" Sarie studied Laurel, holding her gaze for long minutes.

"I thought I would just think about her really hard and concentrate on being with her." Laurel shrugged helplessly. "I'm not sure what else to do."

"Use the talisman the selkie gave you," Coll chimed in.

"Laurel and I talked about that last night. What if using it alerts the Council that we're there and leads them to where we are? It seems like too big a risk," Aisling replied.

"I think I should only use it in an emergency," Laurel agreed.

"I'm more worried about how to find our way home," Gort said.

"That's what I'm for," Sarie said. "My job is to hold the gateway open for you and guide you safely back to this world. That's why my stone disc is different from all of yours. Mine is like a lodestone, it will draw your discs back to it. So, as long as you don't lose yours, you will always be able to find your way home, back to me."

“That’s a relief.” Gort sat back with a sigh.

Aisling came back into the kitchen. “Low tide is at fourteen-ten, that’s ten after two this afternoon.”

“Right then, Emily and I will come out with you and guard the gateway. You’ll only have four, maybe four and a half hours, in this time to find them and come back. The times between high and low tide are about six hours. Emily and I won’t be able to stay at the portal once the water gets too high. As it is, we’re going to be pretty cold.”

“What happens if we can’t get back in time?” Coll’s face flushed deep red with anxiety.

“In that case you will have to wait for the next low tide, Emily and I will get out there as soon as the water recedes enough,” Sarie sounded confident, but Laurel noticed the lines of worry on her face.

“We’ll just make sure we’re back in time, that’s all,” Laurel declared.

“I think the best way to ensure your success is to keep in physical contact with each other, holding hands like you did on school outings when you were young. All of you focus on Bella, don’t divide your concentration between her and the selkie. Where she is, he’ll be too.’ Sarie hesitated and looked at Laurel. “You need to be prepared that Bella may not want to come back with you. She may decide to stay with Vear Du, regardless of the danger.”

“I’ll make her understand she needs to come home with me,” Laurel said staunchly. “I know she’ll see reason, I just know it.”

Sarie sighed, but didn’t say anything else on the subject. Instead she began to clear the table.

“We’ll wash up,” Aisling volunteered. She threw a dish towel at the boys. “You can dry.”

“While you lot are taking care of that, I’ll run into Penzance and collect Emily and some things we’ll need for this afternoon,” Sarie declared, heading to the door.

Laurel watched the car disappear down the lane from the window over the sink as she rinsed the plates. Coll came and stood behind her and put his hands on her shoulders. She glanced up at him over her shoulder.

"I'm scared, Coll. What if something goes wrong? I should go by myself, there's no need for all of you to risk it."

"We've been through that before. Remember out at the Men an Tol that night when you thought you'd go off without us?" he reminded her. "We all go, and that's final."

She glanced at Aisling and Gort, hoping they were on her side. The stubborn set of Ash's chin and the determined expression on Gort's face told her she was defeated. Sighing, she handed the last plate to Coll and let the water out of the sink.

* * *

It was just gone one in the afternoon by the time the group reached the high headland of Carn les Boel. A strong wind swept across the cliff face and a falcon soared along the rocks below them. The Atlantic sparkled blue and white in the sun as the surf broke over the base of the cliff. Without speaking, Sarie and Emily turned and led them down the trail over the shoulder of the hill bounded on both sides by purple heather and golden blooming gorse. The coconut-vanilla scent of the gorse seemed out of place with the dread in Laurel's heart. By the time they reached the bottom of the steep descent the tide was fully out. She followed Coll down the wooden steps set into the rock below the little waterfall that ran into Nanjizal bay. The sand was firm underfoot when she reached the bottom. To her left the high, narrow slit in the rock loomed like a formidable foe. It's only a rock, she reassured herself. No, it's not, her common sense screamed, it's a freaking portal to God knows where! As if sensing her rising panic Coll reached over and twined his fingers with hers.

"We'll find them, Laurel. You know we will."

Not trusting herself to speak, she nodded and followed Emily across the beach, picking her way among the rocks littering the sand. When they reached the base of the rock, she halted and moved out of the way as Emily and Sarie made their preparations. At any other time, Laurel would have been interested in just what exactly they were doing and the reasoning behind it. Today, she only hoped they knew what they were doing. Aisling came up beside her and took her other hand. Gort had Aisling's hand firmly in his. Laurel almost laughed. *Just like school kids*. Except this was no school outing, this was a different kind of adventure, and one that could have deadly consequences. She tipped her head back and looked up at the apex of the opening high over her head. Was the portal that big, or did it only take up a small part of the opening? She wished she'd thought to ask Sarie earlier. Right now she didn't want to distract the two women from the arrangement of their tools. She swallowed hard and smiled at Coll.

Pushing her fear to the back of her mind, she dug her feet into the sand and thought of the crystal mare that carried her along the moon paths to Glastonbury Tor when Mom was so sick. The thought gave her confidence.

"Right then, are you lot ready?" Sarie's voice cut through Laurel's thoughts.

She glanced at her friends and nodded. "Whenever you are," she replied. "Any idea how we make this thing work?"

"Let's just concentrate on your gramma and walk through. See what happens," Aisling suggested.

"Okay." Laurel shrugged. She led the way, hesitating only slightly before entering the cleft in the rock. The sound of the waves on the beach was intensified by the close confines. She wrinkled her nose as the scent of wet rock, damp sand, and seaweed surrounded her. She turned to see if they all fit inside the opening and then waited. Closing her eyes, she thought as hard as she could about Gramma Bella. Nothing changed that she could tell. Laurel opened her eyes and stepped all the way through the cleft and out the other side.

"Are we there?" Coll still had his eyes screwed tightly shut.

"We're still where we started, you git." Gort nudged him with his shoulder.

Laurel ignored them, frustration rising in her chest. What were they doing wrong? "Let's go back through from this side. Maybe that will make a difference." She walked boldly into the shadow of the towering stone and out the other side where Sarie and Emily kept watch.

"Any suggestions?" Laurel asked Sarie.

"Gather round and let me smudge you lot. I included you when I did the site earlier, but perhaps this will do the trick."

They gathered in a circle by the cleft while Sarie and Emily wafted the hallowed smoke about them. "It's thyme for bravery and courage, and lavender for cleansing of thought and intent," Emily told them. Gort sneezed when the pungent smoke curled around his head. For good measure, Sarie drew a circle of sea salt in the sand encompassing their little group and the spire of stone.

"Right, then. Concentrate hard and try again when you're ready," Sarie instructed them, returning to her place beside Emily.

"Ready?" Laurel glanced around at her friends. Fixing an image of Gramma Bella firmly in her mind, she moved toward the cleft once more. Her steps faltered just before the entrance as a wave of dizziness swept over her and the air seemed to ripple in the depths of the shadows. Coll didn't stop in time and ran into her, pushing her forward.

"Go back, go back!" A thin reedy voice sounded from the thin air in front of her.

"Wait, something's wrong," Emily cried at the same time.

"Stop, stop! Don't enter here." Gwin Scawen materialized in mid-air and dropped to the sand at Laurel's feet. He scrambled to his feet and snatched up his hat that had fallen in the sand. "You can't go through this portal." He gasped for breath.

Aisling dropped to her knees by the little man. "Slow down and catch your breath." The piskie sagged against her, his thin limbs trembling. When his breathing had slowed, he looked up at Aisling.

"Thank the Lady I got here in time to stop you," his voice still quavered.

"Why? What's wrong, Gwin?" Aisling prompted him.

"You can't use this portal, it's far too dangerous," he insisted.

"What's wrong with it? Gramma used it and it worked for her," Laurel demanded. "Did something happen to her? Is she hurt?" A horrible thought occurred to her.

"Peace, no, no. She is fine for the moment," Gwin assured her.

"Fine, then it will work for us too." Laurel moved toward the rock.

Gwin threw himself at her legs and hung on. "You cannot, Mistress Laurel. You must not."

She looked down at the bedraggled piskie impatiently. "We don't have time for this. Cut the crap and just tell me why we can't go through here."

"Yes, yes, of course." He drew a deep breath and Laurel glowered at him. "Patience is a virtue, Mistress Laurel," he said tartly.

"Gwin Scawen, you tell me what you're on about right this minute or I'm going through," Laurel threatened.

"No, no, you can't, you mustn't." He blanched beneath the swarthy tone of his face.

"Why not?" she growled.

"They're watching the portal…if you go through here you won't get two feet before they have you in their net," he said.

"They who?" Coll asked.

"The Council's men. They can't locate the selkie and his mate, but they know you are planning to come through and they're waiting."

"What good will we be to them?" Laurel edged closer to the rock.

"They plan to use you as bait to lure their quarry out of hiding. Blood calls to blood."

"Laurel, listen to reason." Sarie pulled her further away from the cleft.

She chewed her lower lip in frustration and paced in circles. She stopped abruptly. "Is there another portal nearby that we can use?" Laurel looked from the piskie to Emily and Sarie.

"It's what I came to tell you," Gwin stood up and spread his arms wide in an expansive gesture.

Laurel ground her teeth. "Couldn't you have just started with that instead of beating around the bush?"

"I was getting to it," Gwin defended himself.

"Where is the portal? We've wasted the better part of two hours here and the tide is turning. If it's on the coast, time is running out for this afternoon." Sarie looked toward the sea where the wind was whipping spindrift from the tops of the waves.

"No need to worry about the tides, Mistress Sarie. No need at all." Gwin capered around them, coat tails flying behind him.

"Where do we need to go, then?" Ash asked.

"To the stone circle," he announced proudly.

Laurel groaned inwardly. "Which circle? The one near the Men Scryfa, the Nine Maidens?"

"No, no, no." The piskie shook his head and danced around Aisling.

"The Merry Maidens?" Coll suggested.

"No, no, no." Gwin danced faster, twirling his pointed hat.

"Stop being silly and be serious for a moment, please." Ash caught his hand as the piskie whirled by her.

"As you wish, keeper of my heart." He stopped dancing and bowed low, the tip of his nose brushing the sand, his long forelock swinging in the sea wind.

"Thank you. Now, please tell me what stone circle you think we can use as a portal," Aisling coaxed.

"The circle with the pointing finger and the white quartz marker, of course." Gwin appeared astounded at her puzzlement.

Laurel glanced at her friends and then at Sarie and Emily. Surely, one of them would know what the piskie was talking about.

"He means Boscawen-un Stone Circle," Emily exclaimed.

"Yes, yes, yes. That is what you know it as. Boscawen-un." Gwin capered around them again.

"Is it near here?" Laurel looked up at the cliffs.

"It's a fair piece," Emily said.

"How far?" Laurel asked, keeping in mind her idea of a long way was far different than her friends.

"It's north of Saint Buryan, just east of Lower Leha. The stones are quite close to the road, only a short walk in." Sarie said.

"We went through Saint Buryan on the way here, didn't we? It had the old church with the big tower?" Laurel tried to remember how long it took to get to Polgigga after they passed it.

"Yes, we did. There's a narrow road that goes north from there, but I think we should go home first and decide the best way to go about this." Sarie began to gather her things.

"I don't want to wait. Why can't we go there now?" Laurel grumbled.

"Act in haste, repent at your leisure," Emily counselled.

"Yes, yes, best to have a good plan," Gwin agreed.

Laurel opened her mouth to protest and then snapped it shut. Once Sarie made up her mind there was no sense wasting her breath arguing. She bent and helped replace things in the carry all.

Gwin stopped dancing in mid-step and cocked his head to one side. "Coming, I'm coming," he shouted and dived into the shimmer that appeared in the shadowy cleft of rock. He disappeared in a puff of displaced air.

"Sure," Laurel grumbled. "He can use the thing, but we can't." After one last glance at the place he vanished she followed the others up the wooden steps to the path.

On the way back to the layby, they took the easier path up the little valley cut by the stream rather than the steep climb back up the cliff to Carn les Boel. The grazing cows regarded her with interest as she passed. They seemed disinclined to do anything other than look, so after a quick glance, Laurel ignored them. She turned to look back down at Nanjizal Bay. The sand gleamed in the late afternoon sun and far out in the shallow waters over the sand bar three seals played in the waves. She shivered. No matter how beautiful the azure sea looked, it was freezing. Mid-December was way too late for swimming.

Coll came up beside her when the path widened enough to allow it. "At least we don't have to worry about the tide," he attempted to console her.

"I suppose that's true. I just hate waiting, it feels like the longer it takes the less chance we have of finding them."

"If we can get that bloody piskie to stay still long enough, I bet he could take us to them."

"Maybe Ash can get him to help us once we figure out how to make the portal work," Laurel said.

"C'mon," he took her hand and pulled her behind him. "We should catch up to the others."

The walk back to the car took less time than she expected. Soon she was crammed in the back of the car beside Coll. He grinned at her and put his arm around her shoulder. Laurel squirmed so she fit more snugly against his side. She spared a thought for Chance back in Alberta. She was fond of him, but he just wasn't Coll. Laurel made mental note to give Carly a call when she got back to the house. The prepaid phone card Mom sent with her would come in handy for transatlantic calls.

Once they reached Sarie's they all pitched in to unload the car. After a quick meal, Sarie sent them out to look after the horses while she and Emily replenished the items they had used on the beach at Nanjizal.

Laurel paused in the middle of brushing Lamorna's broad black rump. She leaned across the pony's back and looked at Aisling. "Why do you think the portal worked for Gwin and not for us?"

"He's a piskie and we're mortals," Ash spoke through the cloud of dust and hair rising from Ebony's back.

“I suppose…” Laurel resumed brushing the pony.

“Stand on your own feet, you git,” Coll grumbled at Arthur. The Fell pony turned his head and nosed the boy who was bent over cleaning out a front hoof. He set the foot down and straightened up bracing his hands on the small of his back. “So how do we get around the being mortals part?”

“Aren’t there days when it’s supposed to be easier to move from one reality to another?” Gort poked his head up from behind Gareth.

“You might have something there,” Ash agreed.

“You mean like on the night of a full moon, like we did at the Men an Tol?” Laurel started brushing again.

“No. I think he means the quarter days and cross-quarter days of the old calendar.” Aisling narrowed her eyes in thought.

“What are quarter days? And cross-quarter days, they sound religious or something. You mean crosses like in a church?” Coll frowned.

“Not at all. Quarter days marked the Solar Festivals of Alban Eiler, the spring or vernal equinox, Alban Huerin, Summer Solstice, Alban Elved, the fall or autumnal equinox, and Alban Arthuran, Winter Solstice. The Cross-Quarter days were Fire Festivals and linked with the agricultural year. February first is Imbolc, Beltaine is celebrated on May first, Lughnasadh is on August first and Samhain is November first,” Aisling explained.

“It’s almost December twenty-first,” Laurel exclaimed. “Do you think we’d have better luck then?”

“I think it’s likely, but we should ask Emily and Sarie. They’ll know better than I do.”

“You said the cross-quarter days were agricultural. What does that mean?” Gort finished grooming Gareth and came and sat on a bale of hay near Aisling.

“Let me see what I remember…right, then. Imbolc means ewe’s milk and is the time when new lambs are born and the first blades of grass start to show. Beltaine,” she pronounced it Beltanya, “celebrates the start of summer and the end of spring planting. Lughnasadh,” she pronounced it

Loo-nasa, "is the celebration of the start of the harvest. It's named after Lugh Lamfada, a Celtic solar hero or god. Samhain," she pronounced it, "Sow-hen, marks the beginning of winter and the end of harvest. It was also the start of the old Celtic new year. Does that help?"

"Sure, clear as mud," Coll grumbled.

Laurel grinned when Gort made a face at him.

"Good to know, I guess. But what I'm interested in is the winter solstice. It's one of those quarter days, right?" Laurel asked.

Aisling nodded. "It's the longest night and the shortest day of the year. There are old legends about the Oak King of summer fighting with the Holly King of winter. It seems backwards to me, 'cause the Oak King starts to come into power on the winter solstice when the sun starts to regain its strength. But that's the middle of winter and I always think it should be the Holly King who has the upper hand. Except the Holly King gets his chance at power starting at the summer solstice when the sun begins to get weaker and even though it's high summer, the Holly King of winter begins his reign, stealing a bit of the sun's strength every night." She shook her head and went back to brushing Ebony.

"Doesn't really make sense to me," Laurel agreed. "You think we might have better luck on the twenty-first, though?"

"I do, but let's ask when we go back in the house."

Laurel let the subject drop and finished brushing Lamorna. She threw the New Zealand rug over the pony and secured the straps before leading the mare to the door and letting her go. She stepped aside to free up the door for Aisling and Ebony. Arthur and Gareth were already in the pasture nose deep in the grass. Laurel grinned at the sight. Back home any grass would be dry and brown and most likely buried under two feet of snow. She certainly didn't miss the Alberta winter.

Dusk was darkening the sky and softening the edges of the buildings. The warm yellow light spilling from the kitchen windows drew them toward the house. Laurel welcomed the flush of heat that enveloped her when she pushed through the kitchen door from the unheated mud room. Sarie and Emily had spread the table with a cream tea. Her eyes lit up at the sight. It was like a million calories, but she didn't care. There was nothing like a Cornish cream tea.

"Cream tea! Just what we need," Laurel crowed with pleasure.

"We thought it might make up the disappointment this afternoon," Emily said.

"If you'd been successful, it was going to be a celebration," Sarie added.

Laurel glanced at Ash.

"Would it be better to try at Boscawen-un on the twenty-first?" Aisling looked from Emily to Sarie.

"It's winter solstice," Laurel said helpfully.

"I do know that." Sarie gave her a wry look and Laurel had the grace to blush.

"Sorry," she muttered.

"All joking aside, it might be just the thing," Emily said.

"When's the best time? Noon hour, or sunset maybe?" Coll asked.

"What about dawn? Oh wait, that means getting up early," Gort teased him.

Coll glowered at him.

"Actually, according to the old traditions, the new day starts on sundown of what we would consider the day before. So, reckoning that way, the twenty-first starts at sundown on the twentieth," Emily explained.

"That's just weird." Laurel screwed her face up.

"What time is the actual moment when the sun reaches its southern most point?" Sarie asked.

"I'll look it up, just a second." Coll brought up the information on his cell phone. "According to this it's at sixteen-thirty-four UTC on the twenty-first."

"What does UTC mean?" Laurel was confused, she'd never heard the term before.

"Isn't it the same as Greenwich Mean Time?" Aisling looked at Emily for confirmation.

“That’s right. But UTC stands for Co-ordinated Universal Time, it’s basically replaced Greenwich Mean Time as the twenty-four hour time standard which is kept by highly precise atomic clocks,” she explained.

“It should be just about sunset which will make things much easier than if it was in the middle of the night,” Sarie sounded satisfied with the fact.

“Sixteen-thirty- four is…” Laurel counted off the hours on her fingers, “…four-thirty-four in the afternoon. Almost twenty-five minutes before five.”

“Let’s plan to be ready at that exact time then,” Sarie said. “We’ll need to get there beforehand to get things set up and for you lot to prepare yourselves.”

“Should we go out tomorrow and take a look around. I don’t think I’ve ever been to that circle,” Gort suggested.

“I’ve never been there. The only stone circle I’ve been to is the Hurlers. I wanted to visit the Merry Maidens last time, but with everything else that happened there was never enough time,” Laurel said. “I think I’d feel more confident about being able to activate the portal if I at least had some idea of how things are situated.”

“There’s no reason we can’t take a run out there tomorrow,” Emily agreed. “But for now it’s time to get you boys home. I’m knackered and the next few days will be busy ones to say the least.”

“Off you go, then.” Sarie shepherded Emily and the boys to the door.

“G’night, see you in the morning,” Laurel called as the door closed.

Aisling waved before starting to gather up the odds and sods off the table. “It has been a long day.” She smothered a yawn. “I’m glad I’m staying the night here.”

“How did you get your mum to agree to let you stay?” Laurel paused in wiping down the table and glanced at her friend over her shoulder.

“Dad said it was only fair since I asked you to come for the holidays and then Mum’s old auntie showed up and took over my room so there’s no bed for either of us. He convinced her there was no way we could expect a guest to sleep on the sofa in the parlour." She giggled. "I was never so glad to see Great Auntie Astrid in my life. I hate sharing a room with her, she snores, and she farts something awful."

"Aisling!" Sarie pretended to be appalled. "That's no way to speak about your elders."

"Sorry, Sarie." She dipped her head and winked at Laurel.

"Off to bed with you, now. Up you go and leave the hall light burning. I've a few things to do before I come up."

Laurel pushed through the door to the hall and held it for Aisling. At the bottom of the stairs she stopped and looked back toward the kitchen. "What do you suppose she's doing?"

Aisling shrugged. "Maybe something to do with us getting the portal to work properly, she might be reading the tarot cards or something."

"I'd like to sneak back and watch." Laurel cocked her head and chewed her bottom lip.

"Curiosity killed the cat, remember," Aisling said. "If she wanted us to know she wouldn't have chased us out of the kitchen and besides I'm too tired to care right now." She started up the steep stairs.

Laurel hesitated a moment longer and then followed her. She decided she and Ash could talk about their own strategy for activating the portal once they were in bed. By the time she was snuggled under the quilts, the day caught up with her and she fell asleep before she could start a conversation.

Chapter Fifteen

The December morning was bright and clear, the sun burning off the last of the fog and mist by the time Laurel and Aisling finished with the horse chores. They met Sarie on the garden path as she emerged from the hen house with a basket of fresh eggs.

"I'll hard boil some of these and we can have egg salad sandwiches for tea after we come back from the stones," Sarie greeted them. "How are the ponies this fine morning?"

"All good," Laurel replied. She held the door open for the older woman when they reached the house.

"Emily and the boys should be here in a bit," Aisling said. She busied herself laying out plates and juice glasses on the table.

Laurel finished drying the last plate and placed it on the stack in the cupboard when Emily pulled into the yard. She wiped her hands and hung the towel on the rack to air dry. Aisling beat her to the door. She grabbed her jacket and followed her out into the bright sunlight.

"You lot ready to go?" Emily asked Laurel, ignoring Gort and Aisling with their heads together a few feet away.

"Uh huh, Sarie's just getting a few things and said she'll be right out."

"Are we taking two cars? Can I drive?" Coll stuck his head out the driver's side window.

"It might be a good idea." Sarie emerged from the house with a large basket and some rugs in her arms. "I'm not sure how we're going to fit all this into the boot and if we put it on the rear seat there won't be room for all of you."

"Laurel can ride with me," Coll suggested. "You can pile all the extra stuff in the rear."

She grinned and went around to the passenger door. "Is it okay with you, Sarie?" Coll leaned over and unsnibbed the door, pushing it open. Laurel stood with one foot in the car waiting for the older woman to answer.

"Go on with you, then. Just mind you don't dawdle and keep us waiting."

Laurel slid into the seat and closed the door before anyone could change their mind. Coll reached over and squeezed her hand. "I don't think we've hardly been alone since you got here."

"I know." She returned the pressure of his fingers and leaned her head back on the seat, smiling at him.

"Have you figured out a way to make that portal thing work?" He slid the car into gear and followed Sarie's car down the lane.

"I was so beat last night I fell asleep before I could talk to Ash about it." She shook her head. "We could sure use Gwin Scawen's help."

"Maybe he'll show up at the stones," Coll suggested.

"I hope so." She lapsed into silence, staring out the window as they skirted Penzance. She closed her eyes as Coll approached the roundabout near Heamoor. "How can you drive through this thing? I'd be stuck on it going in circles forever."

Coll shrugged. "You just follow the arrows on the pavement and take the exit you want."

Laurel heaved a sigh of relief as the car exited and shot off toward the smaller roundabout where the A30 met the A3071. There was less congestion on this one and Laurel managed to keep her eyes open.

"Where's Sarie?" She peered ahead trying to spot the blue car on the winding road.

"Way ahead of us. I promised Gramma I'd be careful and not drive over the speed limit."

"This is you driving *slow*?"

He nodded without taking his eyes from the traffic in front of him.

“Remind me to never ride with you when you’re planning to drive fast,” she muttered.

“There’s Crows-an-Wra, the layby is just up ahead a bit,” Coll broke the silence.

Laurel sat up straighter and watched for Sarie’s car on the shoulder ahead. “There it is.” She pointed to the muddy layby that came into view as they rounded a slight curve in the road.

Coll pulled in behind the other vehicle, squeezing into the small space so nothing protruded onto the motorway. The others were waiting outside Sarie’s car. Laurel joined them, eager to see the stone circle for herself. They went single file between the gate posts with the name carved into them, and followed the path through the brambles and bracken.

“What does Boscawen-un mean?” She spoke to Sarie who was directly in front of her.

“House of the Elder Tree.”

Laurel glanced around as she left the path and came out into a grassy clearing. “There aren’t even any trees here. Just bushes.”

“There used to be a forest of elder trees surrounding the circle a long, long time ago,” Emily said.

Laurel followed the muddy track that led through a break in the circle of stones. It brought her to the central stone that was set at what she guessed was close to a forty-five degree angle. Approaching it, she laid a hand on it to steady herself as she peered under the foot of the stone where someone had left offerings of some kind. A jolt of electricity shot through her and she jumped back with a muffled screech.

“The thing just gave me a shock.” She shook her hand to ease the tingling.

“It shouldn’t have.” A frown creased Sarie’s face. “I’ve touched it hundreds of times and never had anything happen.”

“Go ahead and see if this time it’s different.” Laurel eyed the stone needle suspiciously.

Sarie went forward and tentatively placed her fingers on the slope of the stone. Nothing unusual happened. “You try,” she said to Emily motioning her forward.

One by one the others touched the stone but there was no repeat of the shock Laurel received. “You try it again,” Aisling suggested. “Maybe it was just static electricity, you know, like scuffing your feet across a rug.”

Laurel stepped near the stone, being careful to stand in a different place than the first time. Her fingers no sooner hovered over the granite than a spark arced from it to her hand. “Ow!” She drew her hand back and sucked on her finger to stop the sting. “I guess it just doesn’t like me.”

“Or maybe it *does* like you,” Gort said. “You might be the key to making the portal work, Laurel.”

“But other than it giving me a shock nothing happened. No doorway opened or anything,” Laurel disagreed.

“Perhaps the timing isn’t right, or we haven’t prepared properly,” Emily said.

“I’m not crazy about the idea of getting zapped by the stupid rock every time I go near it,” Laurel complained.

The breeze that up until then had been blowing in from the sea strengthened into a blustery wind and changed direction. Clouds scurried across the blue of the sky playing hide and seek with the sun. “Looks like we might get blow.” Coll tipped his head back and studied the sky.

“Let’s get to it, then, before it gets any more nippy.” Sarie opened a notebook she pulled from her knapsack. There are nineteen stones situated here, here and here…” She sketched the location of the stones in relation to each other. “The central stone is unusual, most circles don’t have one in the centre.”

“How come it’s tipped over? Is it getting ready to fall down?” Laurel asked.

Sarie shook her head and kept sketching. “No, it’s been that way for as long as anyone knows. There’s a lot of speculation it was meant to be that way from the beginning.”

“Why?” Laurel walked around the stone being careful not to get too close.

"Nobody knows for sure. Hamish Miller dowsed the circle and found that the earth energy line changed direction when it came to the stone and went off across country at the same angle as the stone. Like it was placed there to divert the energy for some reason," Emily said.

Sarie glanced up at the position of the sun. "The stone faces the north-east…" She made more notations in the notebook. "Coll, can you go stand by the quartz stone, please?"

He looked around in confusion until Emily pointed toward a stone and nodded. Coll moved to stand behind it and looked more closely at it. "Hey, it is different than the others. Look at that!"

Sarie made more notes on her page. "The quartz stone is in the west-south-west of the circle. If I remember correctly it is supposed to mark the sunrise on Beltaine." She walked around the stones stopping to make observations in her book at each one.

Coll leaned a hand on the quartz stone and jumped back with a shout.

"What happened?" Laurel hurried over to him.

"Bloody thing bit me," he exclaimed. "It gave me a shock just like that one did you." He nodded toward the central stone.

"Now, that's interesting, so it is." Sarie came over to join them. She stood in front of the quartz stone and paced off the distance to the pointing finger in the centre. She stopped as she reached the tilted menhir, the tapering length sloped up and away from where she stood. "I wonder if this is the secret to opening the portal?"

"What do you mean?" Gort joined her.

"Come here and look, all of you." She motioned for the rest to gather around her. "If the quartz stone reacts to Coll, I think we can assume it likes the male energy, and if the central stone reacts to Laurel, it must be attracted to her feminine energies."

"Doesn't that make the quartz male and the menhir female? It makes no sense, the tilted stone is so obviously a male symbol of fertility," Emily argued.

Sarie shook her head. "No, the white quartz is female which is why it reacts to the opposite male energy, and the same for the centre stone. It is male and reacts to Laurel's female energies."

"But why won't it react to me then?" Aisling laid her hand on the stone needle.

"I don't know," Sarie admitted.

"Saying that all that is true, how does it make the portal open?" Gort asked.

"Haven't figured that out yet." Sarie studied her drawings and notes.

"What if the quartz stone powers the needle stone…" Coll began.

"And the tilted one acts as a springboard or a ramp," Laurel broke in. "Remember how when we went through the Men an Tol we actually ended up above the stone…Maybe this will work the same way."

"It might at that." Sarie considered the possibility.

As she finished speaking a clear beam of sunlight broke through the clouds and illuminated the angled stone with a golden glow.

"Can we try it right now?" Aisling fairly danced in place with excitement.

"We aren't prepared, and I think it is wiser to come back tomorrow at the moment of the winter solstice and try it then," Sarie advised.

"I agree," Laurel said. "I'm not ready to do it right now."

As if in agreement, the wind picked up and a cold rain swept across the long grass, tossing the branches of the sheltering bushes. Laurel shivered and pulled the collar of her jacket up. Shoving her hands deep in her pockets, she crossed the circle giving the centre stone a wide berth. Without a backward glance she headed back down the muddy path to the cars. When she reached them she waited impatiently, huddling in the lee of the vehicles. Coll appeared from the bushes first. He unlocked the door and opened it for her. Laurel got in and wrapped her arms around her body for warmth. A blast of rain and wind chilled the interior further when Coll joined her. He slammed the door and blew on his hands before starting the car. With the heat turned on full, they waited for the others to appear.

"What do you think about all that?" Coll tipped his head toward the stone circle hidden now behind the brambles and bushes.

"It's freaking spooky if you ask me. Why do those stupid rocks only shock you and me? I'm scared to death to come back here tomorrow evening."

Coll caught her cold hand in his. "Me, too. Are we supposed to be a sacrifice or something? It electrocutes us and then opens the door for the others?"

She gasped at his words. "Do you really think that's what going to go down? Really?"

"I don't know, Laurel. Sarie knows more than she's letting on, I'm sure of it." Coll squeezed her hand.

"Damn, I wish I could talk to Gramma Bella. Why'd she have to go running away into some other world without me?"

"She loves the seal man and it's been a long time since she's seen him," Coll answered. "If the Council has banned her from seeing him, maybe this is the only way she thinks she can be with him."

"Sarie always said how crazy she was when they were young. Always chasing some wild idea or something…" her voice broke. "Didn't she even think about me?"

"Ah, Laurel…I bet she did, but just got all caught up with wanting to be with the selkie."

Coll leaned closer and she raised her face to meet him. His lips were gentle at first, but when she didn't pull back the pressure increased and became more demanding. The touch of his tongue on her lower lip startled her into opening her eyes. A bolt of heat shot through her. Kissing Chance never felt like this. Closing her eyes she moved nearer to Coll's warmth, the gear shift poking her ribs.

A sharp rap on the window broke them apart. Gort's grinning face looked in at them. "You better look sharp, Sarie and Emily are right behind us."

Laurel sat back and ran her fingers through her messy hair. Her face was hot and she knew her cheeks were red. She blew out a shaky breath and smiled shyly at Coll. There was no chance to say anything as the rest of the group arrived. Gort pulled the rear door open and got in, Aisling joined him.

"Sarie says for us to ride with you on the way back. She wants to talk to Emily without 'little ears' hearing everything." Aisling pulled a face.

"More like she wants to keep these two apart," Gort teased, reaching forward and poking Coll in the ribs.

Laurel glanced over at him and almost burst out laughing. Coll's face was so red it looked like he was on fire. She put her cold hands up to her own hot cheeks. The ride home was silent, except for the whispering of Gort and Ash in the rear. They spoke too low for Laurel to make out anything they were saying.

The remainder of the day passed in a blur for Laurel. She wavered between worrying about what was going to happen the following day and thinking about kissing Coll. When it was finally time for bed she lay awake staring at the ceiling unable to shut off the turmoil of her thoughts.

"Ash, are you awake?" she whispered.

"What?" Ash replied.

"I can't sleep."

"Me neither."

"What was going on with you and Coll in the car? It looked pretty intense." Aisling propped herself up on an elbow and looked down at Laurel.

"What did it look like?" She avoided answering, her whole body was hot.

"C'mon, Laurel. Spill."

"Okay. He kissed me…and I kissed him back."

"Is that the first time you've snogged with him? What was it like?"

"It's the first time he's kissed me like that. It made me feel all mushy inside."

Aisling giggled. "Mushy?"

"I guess, I don't know how else to describe it. What's it like when Gort and you make out?"

"We don't exactly 'make out', as you put it. But I guess being with him makes me all squidgy inside," Aisling confessed.

"Squidgy?" Now it was Laurel's turn to laugh.

"Has that bloke back home, Chance, has he ever snogged you?"

"A couple of times after a school dance, and once at a tailgate party, but he seemed to enjoy it more than me."

"Did you tell him that?"

She shook her head. "No, I couldn't."

"Why ever not? It's not fair if you don't feel the same way he does."

"It's complicated. Carly is my best friend and Chance is her brother. We've been friends forever, it's just the last couple of years things have changed between me and him. He's always around when I'm over at their place."

"Still, you should let him know."

"It's not like I'm stringing him along or anything," Laurel protested.

"I guess you can't really control how he feels. As long as you're not encouraging him."

"I'm more worried about what's going to happen when we try to open that portal tomorrow."

"It's weird that those stones only react to you and Coll. That's just spooky," Ash agreed.

"I'm not even sure how I'm going to find Gramma Bella. What if I get us all lost?" Laurel chewed her lower lip.

"If worse comes to worse, you can use that talisman. It should take you straight to Vear Du, and us with you," Ash reassured her.

"Do you think it will even work once we go through? Assuming Coll and I can key the portal."

"I think we need to quit worrying and surround ourselves with positive thoughts. Emily says you run into whatever you carry in with you."

"What?" Laurel sat up and stared at Aisling.

"It means if a person is thinking bad thoughts or feeling angry, that's what will be drawn to you when you travel into the other worlds. So we need to concentrate on going straight to wherever it is your gramma and Vear Du are."

"I guess that makes some kind of sense." Laurel slid back down under the quilt.

"Let's try and sleep, okay. Tomorrow is gonna be a long day." Aisling rolled over.

Laurel stared at the cracks in the ceiling and watched the shadows gather in the corners of the room. *Gramma Bella, where are you?* The thought repeated over and over until her eyelids grew heavy and she drifted off.

Chapter Sixteen

Laurel chewed on her thumbnail and glanced at Coll seated beside her in the rear of the car. His face was pale and his Adam's apple bobbed as he swallowed. He caught her gaze and slid his hand over hers.

"It's gonna be okay, Laurel. We managed to survive the star paths the last time when your mum was sick."

She nodded, not trusting her voice to speak. Possibilities skittered across her mind, most of the scenarios ending in disaster. *Think positive, think positive. Remember what Ash said, I have to think positive thoughts.* The wipers pushed the water around on the windscreen, but did little to improve the visibility. The stormy weather was doing nothing to improve her mood.

Sarie pulled into the rain-soaked layby and turned off the ignition. Laurel peered through the water sluicing down the window, watching for Emily's vehicle to join them. The thought of going out into the downpour was daunting. She wriggled her cold toes in the borrowed rainboots.

"Here she is," Sarie announced as Emily's car splashed to a halt behind them.

"Great," Laurel muttered.

Coll grinned and squeezed her hand. Pulling up the hood of his mac to ward off the rain, he opened the door and ducked out. Laurel sighed and jammed an old hat of Sarie's onto her head. There was nothing for it but to brave the weather and get on with it. She emerged into the storm, turning her back to the wind. Emily handed her a waterproof basket and smiled at her. Laurel clutched it like a lifeline to hide her trembling hands. Once the boots of both cars were empty, Sarie led the way toward the gate, the sign post gleaming bleakly in the driving rain. Laurel pushed the water soaked brambles away as she slogged through the mud in the deepening gloom.

"Who are we supposed to know when sunset is in this muck?" she muttered.

"It doesn't matter if we can see the sun or not, I've got my watch set to the atomic clock so we'll know the exact moment the solstice occurs. The tipping point between the death and rebirth of the sun," Sarie remarked over her shoulder.

Laurel shivered at the words death and rebirth. A cold finger that had nothing to do with the rain slithered down her spine. She left the dubious shelter of the brambles and bushes that bordered the path and stood near the gap in the circle that served as an entrance of sorts. Her friends gathered around her. Sarie pushed her sleeve back and checked her watch.

"We have a bit of time. Emily and I have a few things to take care of before it's your turn to take action."

Laurel huddled next to Coll, Gort and Aisling close by. The wind began to lessen and the rain tapered off a little bit. Sarie and Emily returned from the circuit they had made of the ring of stones.

"Are you ready? It's time to take your places." Sarie put her hand on Laurel's arm.

She nodded and moved to stand at the spot Sarie had marked for her, the angled stone sloped away and upward from her like a ramp. Coll stood behind the white quartz stone being careful not to touch it. Gort and Aisling came to stand between him and Laurel like a living chain.

Sarie's voice counting down the seconds seemed to come from a long way away. Laurel strained to hear it. As the last seconds passed she thought hard about Gramma Bella and reached out to the stone. She clutched Gort's hand, Aisling grasped Coll's arm as he stepped out from behind the quartz. They formed a connection, male and female alternating like a current. Coll touched the quartz with his free hand at the same time Laurel contacted the central needle.

A flash of brilliant light blinded her. Then, just as what happened at the Men an Tol with Gwin Scawen, they stood outside the storm. It still raged around them, but nothing touched them. A golden beam of light touched the quartz stone and illuminated the centre stone. Laurel looked up the sloped ramp and an opening appeared in the heart of the light. Suddenly unafraid, she walked up the angled stone without seeming to touch it and pushed through the flaring light.

The glare faded in a moment and she looked around. The rain swept circle of Boscawen-un was far below her, four odd looking dolls lay sprawled on the grass in a line joining the quartz and centre stone. She turned her face away and looked over the landscape stretching away before her under a sun kissed sky. She was reassured to find that Coll, Gort, and Aisling, were gathered around her. A nebulous silver thread connected them all to the tiny figures of the two women waiting in the rain far below.

Laurel lifted her head and thought very hard about Gramma Bella and Vear Du, picturing them clearly in her mind. She was startled to hear a deep bell tolling, the sound rolling toward her from the south-west.

"It from out in the Scillies," Aisling's voice sounded a long way away. Laurel watched her mouth shape the words moments before the sound reached her ears.

"The Isles of Scilly?"

"We need to go there," Gort spoke in the same disconnected way Aisling had.

"How?" Coll asked.

Gwin Scawen popped into view, clinging to Aisling's shoulder. "Follow me, we can use the Men Omborth to travel there as quick as thought."

"Wha—" Laurel began.

Gwin grinned and in a flash they were standing on a huge granite boulder. The rock began to sway under Laurel's feet. She closed her eyes against the dizzying effect.

"I know where we are," Gort exclaimed. "This is the Logan Rock by Treen Dinas."

"How did we get here?" Coll steadied himself and caught Laurel's arm as the rocking increased underfoot.

"These are the other worlds," Gwin explained. "Travelling between places is as easy as thought."

"Is Gramma Bella out in the Scillies?" Laurel cracked an eye open to look at the piskie.

"Oh yes, Mistress Laurel. And by chance, there is a Logan Rock just near where they hide."

"Can you take us all there?" Aisling looked the little man in the eye. "No nonsense?"

He placed a hand over his heart and affected a wounded look. "My flower, you wound me to the quick with your question. I would not play you false. Of course, we can all go."

"I think we should sit down," Laurel suggested as the rock underneath her increased its gyrations. The whole boulder vibrated and a high pitched whine rattled her bones. She sat down rather suddenly, pulling Coll down with her. Gort followed suit. Only Aisling stayed upright, swaying in time with the movement.

"Can you hear the music?" She looked down at them with shining eyes. "It's ever so lovely."

The whine in Laurel's ears increased in volume and the granite grew warm under her. When she thought her head would burst with the intensity of the noise, a huge wave of dizziness swept over her. It was all she could do not to hurl.

The sudden silence made her open her eyes. She didn't remember closing them. Coll's hand was still tightly clasped in hers. Aisling clapped her hands and danced about with Gwin Scawen. Gort looked in every direction as if he didn't know where he was. Laurel raised her eyes and gasped.

They were still sitting on a granite boulder, but not the one near Treen Dinas. This rock was perched on top of a cliff. All around the low island the sea lay like a turquoise blanket. Laurel was reminded of the Caribbean island of Grand Cayman.

"Where are we?" she whispered.

“This is Saint Mary’s. We’re out at the Scillies.” Aisling stopped dancing and looked down at her.

She scrambled to her feet, keeping hold of Coll. He heaved himself up and put a protective arm around her.

“Where are Gramma Bella and Vear Du?” Laurel turned in a full circle.

“They are down in Tom Butt’s Bed,” Gwin announced grandly.

“They’re where?” Laurel was in no mood for riddles or jokes.

“Who is Tom Butt? Gort asked.

“Tom Butt was a boy who didn’t want to be pressed into service on a man o’ war. He hid in a cave for three days and nights. That was back during the reign of Queen Anne.” Gwin Scawen regaled them with the tale.

“So there’s a cave around here somewhere,” Coll said.

“Indeed, and indeed, there is,” Gwin agreed. “Come, it is just a little way down the slope here.”

Gort eyed the steep hill, the way down covered with treacherous rocks. “Is it safe?”

“You will all be unscathed as long as you are with me,” the piskie assured him.

Aisling followed the little man as he picked his way down the slope. Gritting her teeth, Laurel went after her. Coll and Gort brought up the rear. When Gwin was almost down to the level of the sea, he suddenly disappeared. She heard Coll curse behind her and she silently echoed his words. Trust the little trickster to lead them somewhere and then just up and disappear.

“Come on,” Ash called from below. She was too far ahead and past some outcropping rocks to be visible.

Laurel scrambled the last few yards, ending up dirty and dishevelled beside Aisling. They were perched on a narrow ledge with a crumbling lip.

“Is this it?” Laurel fought to control her frustration and rising anger.

“Almost there,” Aisling said gaily. She took Laurel’s hand and led her around the shoulder of another boulder. A low opening yawned black in the cliff face.

“Welcome to Tom Butt’s Bed.” Gwin Scawen bowed deeply, his long nose touching the earth.

“Laurel!” Gramma Bella appeared in the opening.

“Gramma!” Laurel threw herself into the woman’s arms. “Are you okay? Why did you go away? Why didn’t you take me with you?” Her words came out all jumbled and running together. She finally drew a deep breath and let it out slowly. “I miss you so much.” Tears made runnels in the dirt on her cheeks. Her grandmother was holding her so tight it was hard to breathe.

“I missed you too, sweet child. But not even for you could I pass up the chance to be with Vear again. I know that’s selfish of me, but there it is. Your father was right about me. I only think of myself when push comes to shove,” Bella spoke into Laurel’s hair.

Laurel hugged her tighter, afraid if she let go the woman would vanish right before her eyes. “Why are you hiding in a cave?” She loosened her hold and stepped back when Gramma Bella did the same. She kept one arm around Laurel’s shoulders.

“I like caves,” Bella said. A small smile played on her lips. “Vear, come see who has come to visit,” she called into the shadows of the cavern.

The tall man ducked his head as he emerged from the darkness. Drops of moisture glistened in his sable hair. “Laurel! Well met, young woman. You’ve grown up some since last I saw you.” He moved swiftly to her side and dropped a kiss on her forehead. He wrapped his arm around Bella’s waist and she smiled up at him.

Laurel’s breath caught in her throat at the look of pure joy radiating from the older woman’s face. She lowered her gaze as a wave of embarrassment washed over her. She felt as if she were spying on something intimate. Coll cleared his throat and coughed behind her. She laid her hand on Vear’s arm.

“Vear Du, this is Coll. He’s Emily’s grandson. And this is Aisling and Gort.”

Gwin Scawen capered about, tiny puffs of sand spurting up in his wake. “Aisling is my own special friend,” he boasted.

Vear smiled indulgently at the piskie before turning his attention to Laurel’s friends. “It’s pleased I am to make your acquaintance.” He bowed his head in acknowledgement of each visitor.

“Oh my, where are my manners? Come, come, sit by the fire and I’ll pour some tea for you.” Bella moved away from the selkie and herded them toward the small fire pit. A number of boulders were pulled up in a circle around it.

“Were you expecting us?” Coll eyed the boulders as if they might jump up and bite him.

“Goodness, no.” Bella laughed. “We are expecting company, but I never dreamed you lot would show up.” She hugged Laurel again. “Come, sit.” She waved her hand to indicate the stones.

Once they were all seated with a mug of hot tea in their hands. Laurel thought to ask just who was coming to visit. “Who are you expecting?”

Bella glanced at Vear who raised one shoulder in a half shrug and nodded.

“You know the Council of Kernow has decreed that we can’t be together, Vear and I,” she paused and looked around the circle of faces. Seeing their confirmation of her statement, she continued. “Given the circumstances it seems a bit unfair and heavy handed, so we have appealed to The Council of Alba, which is really Vear’s home council in any case.”

“I didn’t realize there was more than one council,” Aisling said. Gwin Scawen sat perched on her knee, his twiggy legs crossed.

“Oh yes, each region has its council to see to local affairs. The Grand Council oversees all the local ones. A representative from each local council sits on the Grand Council,” Vear explained.

“What is The Council of Alba?” Coll asked.

“It rules over what in your world is known as Scotland,” the selkie answered.

"How is that your home council when you live in Cornwall?" Coll persisted.

"Selkies are not native to Cornwall but some have migrated down from the cold northern shores of Scotland. However, no matter where we chose to live we are governed by the Council of our birthplace. I was born on the shores of the Calf of Eday, so the Council of Alba is my home Council."

Coll burst out laughing. "The Calf of Eday? Where the bloody hell is that?"

Aisling frowned at him and Gort kicked him in the ankle. "Gerrof, you git." Coll glared at him.

"The Calf of Eday is an island in the Orkneys off the north coast of Scotland. It is a wild and lonely place, but beautiful in its own right." Vear looked over their heads with a faraway look in his eyes.

"Can your Council tell this other Council to let you and Gramma be together?" Laurel squeezed Gramma Bella's hand.

"This is our hope," Bella replied.

"So will you come and live with Gramma in Bragg Creek?" Laurel addressed Vear Du. An uncomfortable silence greeted her words. "What? You're planning on coming home, aren't you?" She turned to Bella.

"I am home," Bella said. The look she exchanged with the selkie seemed to shut out everyone present, as if it were only the two of them in the whole world. Vear's smile seemed to light the whole cave.

"Where are you going to live if you don't come back to Alberta?" Laurel demanded. She didn't like where the conversation seemed to be headed.

"We haven't worked that out yet, but most likely it will be here in Cornwall," Bella said. "I know you probably don't want to hear that, but it is what I desire."

"What about me?" Laurel wailed. "What about Dad? He's pissed at you for lying to him, but he still loves you. You have to come home and make things right with him. He's never changed anything in that cabin you lived in behind our place, you know. He still goes up there sometimes, but he thinks Mom and I don't know that."

"Does he, now?" Vear fixed Bella with a strange look.

Tears stood in Bella's eyes, intensifying the deep blue of the irises. "I'll contact him when all this is done with and see if he is ready to speak to me," she promised.

"You know my feelings on this subject," Vear said. "But that is at least a step in the right direction."

"Getting back to this council thing," Aisling changed the subject, "Is there a chance the decision could be changed? Wouldn't all the councils have equal say in things?"

"I plan to ask the Council of Alba to appeal the decision by the Council of Kernow to the Grand Council. If they agree, I think there is a strong enough case that the sentence will be rescinded," Vear spoke gravely.

"When will all this happen?" Gort piped up.

"I have had word that the Council of Alba has agreed to come down and hear my case. They should be arriving tonight."

"Can we stay and see it?" Laurel asked.

"No, lass. It must be only Bella and myself. And Gwin," he added.

Gwin nodded, the tip of his tall pointed hat bobbing.

The selkie tipped his head and his eyes unfocussed for a moment. "It is time you youngsters were going. You have been journeying long enough and the connection is growing thin."

"But I want to stay and find out what happens. I don't want to leave Gramma." Laurel clung to Bella who stroked her hair.

The deep sonorous tolling of a bell filled the cavern, the rock around them vibrating.

"Your time and place is calling," Gwin said seriously and hopped down from Aisling's knee. Taking her hand, he pulled her to her feet. Gort rose with her. Coll came to stand with Laurel.

"You'll let us know how the meeting goes, won't you?" Laurel looked at Vear.

"Of course, little love. If I can't come myself, if the news is not what I wish it to be, I will send Gwin in my place," he promised.

"We should go." Aisling pulled at her arm.

Laurel nodded. "C'mon, Gramma." She started to follow her friends toward the entrance of the cave.

"I'm not coming with you," Bella's voice sounded choked.

Laurel's heart jumped in her chest, she tried to protest but couldn't seem to get enough breath to form the words. She whirled around and strode back to confront her grandmother. Finally finding her voice she exploded. "What do you mean you're not coming?" Her voice rose unsteadily.

Bella's hand flew to her throat. "Oh my Lord, Laurel! You're the spitting image of my Colton." She sank down onto a boulder. Vear placed a steadying hand on her shoulder.

"I'm beginning to understand why Dad is so mad at you," Laurel spoke through clenched teeth. "How are you supposed to call him and set things right if you don't come back with us?"

"I don't know. I won't know until after the council meeting." Bella's voice grew stronger and she leaned against Vear.

"You promised!" Laurel hissed. How could Gramma betray her like this?

"Laurel, please try to understand. I have to stand with Vear before the Grand Council and face the charges against him, and me, really. It's my fault the Kernow Council is unhappy with him in the first place." Bella pleaded with her granddaughter.

"How does the Council even know who you are?" Laurel crossed her arms and scowled.

Bella sighed and looked up at Vear. "When I first met Vear he used magic in front of me, and to aid me, he broke the rules set by the Council of Kernow. They might have been persuaded to look the other way, but…"

"But I made a grave error in judgement in their eyes. I allowed myself to fall in love with a mortal, and to compound the problem further, against all odds I fathered a child on that mortal," Vear took up the tale.

"It was never a mistake! Don't ever say that. I have no regrets about loving you," Bella declared.

"So if you loved each other so much, why didn't you marry her? Why did you run away?" She addressed the last question to Gramma Bella. Laurel shook off the calming hand Coll placed on her arm. "Leave me alone," she hissed through her teeth.

"Laurel, my little love, it wasn't that simple," Vear began. "As you know, I never realized Bella was with child until many years later, when you yourself told me about your father."

"I was terrified and Da was livid. I thought he was going to kill me, and then he tried to make me marry Daniel Treliving," she glanced at Gort, "there was no way on heaven or earth I would let that man touch me. I was afraid to tell Vear I was pregnant after the way Da acted. I was young, Laurel, and very afraid." Bella reached out her hand and Laurel took a step backward.

"So you lied to your lover, and then you lied to Daddy," she accused.

"I never lied to Vear—" Bella began.

"You never told him the truth either, that's a lie by omission," Laurel maintained, not willing to offer any quarter.

"Laurel, we need to go," Coll sounded desperate.

"You are your father's daughter, that's for sure. Anna was more understanding," Bella said.

"Laurel!" Aisling called urgently. "We need to go, now."

Gwin Scawen scampered over and pulled at Laurel's jeans. She swatted at him with her hand. "I'm coming in a minute." A wave of dizziness made her stagger backward.

"You must go, Laurel. I'm staying with Vear, but I will find a way to come to you and answer whatever questions you have. I love you." Bella hugged her.

Laurel held herself stiffly and didn't return the embrace. She was afraid to speak in case she revealed the tears threatening to choke her. She turned and joined her friends by the entrance to the cave. She took one last look back at Gramma Bella and Vear.

"Go gently," Bella called.

Laurel nodded and stepped out into the light. "How could she do this to me?" She blinked back the tears.

"I don't know. Maybe we'll understand better when we're older," Aisling said. She hooked her arm through Laurel's and drew her onto the narrow path leading up the cliff face.

Laurel scrambled up the steep incline close behind her friends. Coll reached down with his hand and hauled her the last few feet. Gwin Scawen was already perched on the Logan Stone with Gort and Aisling. Coll joined them and Laurel dragged herself up beside him.

"Rock the stone. Rock the stone," Gwin chanted.

"Think of Sarie and Emily," Aisling called as the stone hummed underfoot.

Wild music rose and another wave of vertigo made Laurel close her eyes. She opened them when the song of the rock ended abruptly. They were back on the Logan Stone near Treen Dinas.

"Almost home," Coll said. He gripped her hand, Gort took her other hand. His and Aisling's were entwined as well.

"Can you help us the rest of the way?" Ash smiled at Gwin Scawen.

"Of a certainty, my flower," Gwin replied.

Before Laurel could open her mouth to say anything she was swept up by a strong wind. She worried she would be blown apart as the fingers of wind plucked at her consciousness. Without warning the wind died and the sun shone warm on her shoulders. She was balanced on a point above the angled stone of the Boscawen-un Circle. She glanced around to be sure everyone was with her. Gort, Aisling, and Coll were still joined to her by their connected hands. With a huge sense of relief, Laurel placed her feet on the slanted stone and walked through the brilliant rainbow light. She glanced at the doll-like figures sprawled on the wet grass below her. A vague unease teased at the corner of her mind. Gwin Scawen pulled at her free hand, urging her to move quicker. She hesitated for a moment before giving in to the compulsion to leap from the stone finger. Relief washed over her when she jumped the last few feet. A flash of heat and light blinded her for a moment. The next thing Laurel knew, she was kneeling on the wet grass while the wind and rain beat at her. Raising her head, she saw Coll sitting next to her with his head in his hands. Aisling struggled to her knees and then threw herself at Gort's prone body. Laurel staggered to her feet. Sarie caught her when she would have fallen. Emily helped Coll to his feet, throwing a blanket over his shoulders. Leaving him, she hurried to Gort and Aisling.

"I can't get him to wake up." Aisling was distraught. "Why won't he wake up?"

"I'm here," Gort's voice was thin, as if it came from a long way away.

Ash shoved his upper body up off the ground and supported him against her. Emily wrapped another blanket around both of them. She produced a thermos from under her waterproof cape and offered Gort a container of tea.

"It's just so hard to come back. I'm so happy when I'm with GogMagog in the other worlds. Things are so much easier there." His voice was stronger and more grounded. Aisling released a sigh of relief.

Laurel let Sarie guide her out of the centre of the stone circle. The quartz stone glowed with an iridescent light. When she turned her head to look directly at it, she saw only the rain darkened stone. No light emanated from it. She paused at the break in the circle and looked back. Gwin Scawen danced at the base of the centre stone and then with a series of leaps and bounds that would do an Olympic athlete proud, he popped out of sight. Coll came up on her other side and wrapped his arm around her shoulders.

"We did it, we found your gramma," he whispered in her ear.

"We did, didn't we?" She nodded.

"Come along, you two. Emily will bring the others in a jiffy." Sarie shepherded them out of the clearing and onto the muddy path. Sodden brambles dropped more moisture onto Laurel's clothes. She shivered and almost stumbled. Coll steadied her and she regained her footing.

"Not far now. You must be chilled to the bone." Sarie chivvied them along faster.

Laurel sank into the rear seat with a grateful sigh. Coll shut the door behind him and crowded close to her, spreading his blanket over them both. Sarie started the car and turned the heater on full blast. When Gort and Aisling emerged from the gateway with Emily behind them, Sarie put the car in gear and reversed out of the layby.

"How long were we gone?" Coll asked. "What time is it?"

"About six hours, give or take. It's just gone midnight," Sarie answered.

"That long?" Laurel exclaimed. "It didn't seem like it took so long."

"Time runs different in the other worlds, remember?" Sarie caught her eye in the rear view mirror.

"I suppose."

"Did you find Bella and Vear? I hope your journey wasn't in vain," Sarie said. "My goodness, it's raining cats and dogs." She peered out the windscreen which the wipers failed miserably to clear.

"We did find them," Laurel replied. "Gramma didn't want to come back with me."

"I can't say as I'm surprised. Where the selkie was concerned, Bella never could think straight, or see past her own desires," Sarie said.

Out of habit, Laurel started to defend Gramma Bella, but then stopped. Sarie was right, she realized. And so was Dad. She guessed she owed her father an apology when she got home. He'd tried to tell her and she just hadn't wanted to listen.

“She’s pretty certain she wants to stay with him. But how is that possible? She’s mortal, Vear Du will outlive her.”

“If she stays in the other world she’ll age much slower than a regular mortal. Because time runs differently there it affects how she ages,” Sarie explained.

“But still…”

“Shouldn’t you just be happy that she’s happy?” Coll suggested.

“I guess you’re right.” Laurel wrestled with feelings. She wanted Gramma Bella to be happy where Laurel could be with her, not in some nebulous other world.

Chapter Seventeen

Sarie parked as close to the house as she could. Laurel and Coll dashed through the pelting rain to the mud room door. Sarie joined them seconds later. The lights of Emily's car danced up and down as she negotiated the laneway. The wind howled through trees, the sound sending shivers down Laurel's spine.

Emily parked beside Sarie. The night seemed much darker without the benefit of her head lamps. Laurel and Coll stepped back to make room for Emily and her passengers to come in the narrow door.

"The BBC said on the radio the waves are swamping the Promenade down in Penzance. The water is coming right up to the Lugger." Emily reported while she removed her rain gear and shook the excess water from it.

"If the water's that high, the road by Marazion might be dangerous or impassable. Why don't you all stay here tonight, where it's high and somewhat dry?" Sarie said.

"Aisling, you better ring your folks and tell them where you are so they won't worry," Emily said.

"Mum won't be pleased, but Da will understand," Ash said and pulled her mobile from her jacket pocket. "Bother and damn, it's dead." She glared at the blank screen.

"Try the land line," Sarie suggested. "It might be out too, what with this weather."

Aisling went to use the phone while Laurel trailed after the rest of them into the kitchen. Sarie and Emily soon had a good feed of sandwiches and biscuits on the table along with more tea and coco by the time Aisling returned.

"I got through before the line went dead," she announced. "It looks like there's a message on the machine. The light's blinking," she added.

"I wonder who on earth that could be." Sarie bustled out into the hall to check. She came back a few minutes later with a huge smile on her face. "It was your mum, Laurel—"

"Is everything okay at home," Laurel interrupted her.

"Everything's fine, child. She called to say that her and your dad are coming to England for Christmas. Isn't that wonderful?"

"Dad's coming here?" Laurel squeaked.

"He is. Their flight gets in early tomorrow. All things being equal, they should be here tomorrow evening around six-thirty. They plan to catch the last direct train from Paddington. We'll meet them at the station in Penzance." Sarie rubbed her hands together in excitement.

"This is just brill, isn't it just?" Aisling said. "I get to meet your mum and your dad." She gripped Laurel's hand.

Laurel glanced at Coll who was shovelling food into his mouth. *And Dad will get to meet Coll.* "I wish Gramma Bella had come back with us. I just know I can get Dad to forgive her if he'd just talk to her and let her explain."

"Sometimes it's best to let the hare sit," Sarie said.

"Is that like letting sleeping dogs lie?" Laurel asked.

Sarie nodded. "Now where are we going to put everyone?"

"Mom and Dad can use the spare room across from mine," Laurel said. "Ash can sleep with me until her auntie leaves, and Coll and Gort are at Emily's."

"Where shall we have Christmas supper, your place or mine?" Emily asked.

"We could do Christmas morning at Emily's with the presents and breakfast, and then here for dinner," Laurel suggested. "Ash can come over to Emily's after she's done presents and stuff with her family and then come with us out to the farm. Will your mum be okay with that, do you think?"

"She might let me miss the family dinner if I'm there for the morning. I'll talk to Da first and get him to make her see this is important to me," Aisling said.

"I have to go buy more presents," Laurel exclaimed. "I haven't got anything for Mom and Dad. I left their stuff at home. I brought gifts for you guys, I was gonna give them to you tomorrow before I left."

"If the storm lets up you can shop in the high street when I run into the market in the morning. I'll need to pick up some things too," Sarie said.

"Aisling can help me find what I need." Laurel linked arms with her friend.

"Emily can drop us off at the Wharfside Shopping Centre, by the Animal Charity Shop, we can start there," Aisling said.

Sarie turned on the wireless to listen to the BBC news. The storm was expected to ease off in the morning, although the seas would still be abnormally high and caution was urged in coastal areas.

"I hope the weather will hold for Tom Bawcock's Eve," Coll said.

"Oh that's right! It's tomorrow night, isn't it?" Gort said.

"How wonderful! Colton and Anna will be here in time to enjoy it," Sarie said.

"What's Tom Bobcock's Eve?" Laurel wanted to know.

"Bawcock," Aisling said with a laugh, "Tom Bawcock's Eve, it's a huge celebration at Mousehole harbour. Lots of food and fun and carry on."

"Who is Tom Bawcock? Is he a war hero or something?" Laurel wondered.

"No, I don't think he was ever in the war. Tom was a local Mousehole lad, according to legend. Back in the late nineteenth century, so the story goes, there was a very stormy December and the fishing boats couldn't leave the safety of the Mousehole harbour. Things were very hard in the village, food was scarce and Christmas was just around the corner. On the afternoon of December twenty-third, even though the sea was still raging at the harbour walls and Mount's Bay was churning like a washer woman's tub, your man Tom Bawcock set out to sea. Some of the men folk tried to talk him out of going, and the women stood in the lee of the buildings crying and wringing their hands. No one wanted to mourn a lost fisherman so close to Christmas Day. Tom, he just smiled and cast off his lines and headed out into the storm with his crew. It was getting dark and there was still no sign of his boat coming back into the harbour. Shaking their heads, the men folk retired to the Ship Inn to drink to Tom's health and mourn his supposed demise. A few women kept vigil, those who had lost their men folk to the sea in earlier storms. Just when all hope was lost a great cry went up and Tom Bawcock's fishing boat battled its through the waves and gained the safety of Mousehole harbour. His boat was full to the gunnels with fish and many hands helped him moor his boat and unload his catch. There was plenty for everyone and ever since the people of Mousehole celebrate his bravery with a huge celebration on December twenty-third," Sarie said.

Emily laughed and swatted Sarie on the arm. "You're a good storyteller, my heart. But do remember that there are those who claim the owner of the Ship Inn created the story to boost his custom sometime in the nineteen-fifties."

"Go to sea, you. Robert Norton-Nance wrote about the celebration in nineteen-twenty-seven. It was in the *Old Cornwall* magazine, I think I still have a copy of my mum's upstairs somewhere. He speculated the name actually came from the French *beau coc,* he said the cock was a herald of new light in pagan times and that's where the tradition began," Emily said.

"Who cares about all that old rubbish? What's important is the party!" Coll exclaimed.

"What kind of party, like dancing and stuff?" Laurel's interest was piqued.

"There's a lantern procession down to the harbour, and they turn on the Christmas light display in Mousehole harbour. It's brill, and people come from all over now to see the lights and eat Star-gazey Pie." Aisling danced around the kitchen.

"Star-gazey Pie?" Laurel looked around at her friends for an answer.

“Star-gazey Pie,” Gort giggled, “is a pie made only for the festival. It’s usually a huge thing in a massive dish. It’s made with fish, egg, and potato, with the fish heads sticking up out of the crust. There’s even a book about it called The Mousehole Cat by Antonia Barber,” Gort explained.

“There’s a light display of the Star-gazey Pie down on the sand of the harbour above high tide mark,” Ash added.

“We should teach her the song,” Gort suggested.

“A song? Nope, not a chance, I can’t sing to save my life,” Laurel protested.

“No need to worry about that, the noise is loud. Nobody will hear you anyway and it’s fun to be part of the fun,” Coll assured her.

“Do we have to do it tonight?” Laurel yawned.

“It is getting late.” Sarie glanced at the clock.

“Oh, come on, Laurel. It’s an easy one to learn,” Aisling urged her.

She stood up and motioned Coll and Gort to stand with her. She counted down and they began to sign loudly, swaying from side to side.

“This is the chorus,” Coll shouted. *“Merry place you may believe, Tiz Mouzel ‘pon Tom Bawcock’s eve. To be there then who wouldn’t wesh, to sup o’ sibm soorts o’ fish.”*

“First Verse,” Aisling called. *“When morgy brath had cleared the path, Comed lances for a fry. And then us had a bit o’ scad and Starry-gazie pie.”*

“The chorus,” Coll shouted. They sang the chorus again at the top of their lungs. Sarie and Emily joined in.

“Second Verse,” Gort called. *“As aich we’d clunk, E’s health we drunk, in bumpers bremmen high. And when up caame Tom Bawcock’s name, We’s prais’d ‘un to the sky.”*

“Chorus again,” Sarie called. The kitchen rang with their voices and Laurel joined in, stumbling over some of the unfamiliar words.

They finished with a rousing cheer and Laurel dropped down into a chair, holding her sides from laughing so hard. “What kind of a song is that?”

"Morton-Nance wrote it back in the nineteen-twenties. I think that's why some of the words are so odd," Emily said after she caught her breath.

"I think this calls for some tea." Sarie set the kettle back on the hob and emptied the tea pot before putting in fresh leaves.

"Mom will love this," Laurel said. "She really gets into local customs and stuff. She's always writing down bits of stuff she finds interesting. Says she's going to use it in a book someday." The mention of her mom made Laurel think about her dad and Gramma Bella. Foreboding replaced the hilarity of a moment ago. "When do you think we'll hear anything from Gramma Bella and Vear Du?" Her words sobered the people at the table.

"I'm sure Gwin Scawen will show up the minute anything is decided. He promised me he'd come straightaway once the decision is passed down," Aisling said.

"Do you think they'll come to see us?" Laurel fretted. "I really want Dad to make peace with his mom."

"I think that might be a tall order," Sarie cautioned. "Just because we want something to happen doesn't mean it's the best thing for the people involved."

"If he'd just talk to her and let her explain…" Laurel protested.

"Don't you think she tried to do that when everything came out when you were a child? Colton is as hard headed and stubborn as Bella, he had no interest in her explanations. All he could see was that she lied to him. Your father loved D'Arcy Rowan very much. He was the only father Colton ever knew, so he felt betrayed on two levels. He was angry for D'Arcy and for himself," Sarie continued.

"Did she lie to Grampa D'Arcy too?" Laurel struggled with what she knew was right and her feelings for Gramma Bella.

"No, to her credit, she told D'Arcy the truth. She was pregnant when she landed in Halifax and took the train out here. Bella wrote me soon after she arrived. She was so homesick and pining after the selkie. But she at least had the common sense to tell D'Arcy the truth before she married him. The man was a saint, if you ask me," Sarie explained.

"He was a great grandfather. I miss him so much. I guess I can understand a bit how Dad is so mad at Gramma for lying to him and now running off to be with another man. It's like an insult to Grampa D'Arcy..." Laurel's voice trailed off.

"Why don't you wait until your parents get here and see how it goes? There's no sense in getting in a barney with your Da over something you have no control over," Gort suggested.

"You're probably right. Mom always says I need to be more patient. Just because I think something should happen, doesn't mean it's meant to be that way. She says sometimes I remind her of Gramma Bella when I get my mind set on something," Laurel agreed.

Emily stood up and gathered the mugs from the table and carried them to the sink. Sarie stood as well and wiped the table with a wet cloth.

"Time for bed. Morning comes early and we've a big day ahead of us tomorrow what with Anna and Colton coming and the hooley over in Mousehole later," Sarie declared.

Laurel and Aisling went up the stairs side by side behind the two boys. She stopped on the landing, the boys blocking the way. Gort sidled over to Aisling and kissed her cheek.

"Night, Ash," he whispered so low Laurel almost didn't hear him. His face flushed red and his eyes were bright. "Happy almost Christmas."

"Night, Gort," she replied and kissed him lightly on the lips.

Laurel smothered the urge to laugh when bright flags of colour appeared on his cheeks. She turned to follow Aisling into their room when Coll's hand on her arm halted her. She looked up at him in surprise. His back was to the hall light, his face falling into shadow. She held her breath as he leaned closer, drawing her nearer with the hand on her arm. "Coll?" she whispered, forgetting Gort and Ash were watching. Her vision narrowed until all she could see was Coll's eyes gleaming in the dim light. She took a step closer and tipped her head back as his lips came nearer. He hesitated, his mouth hovering so close she could feel his breath on her skin. A sensation she couldn't identify sent mouse paws skittering down her spine. She stretched up on tip toe to close the gap between them. His lips were softer than she expected but the beginnings of whiskers on his chin pricked her skin. She moved to wrap her arms around his waist in answer to her desire to be closer to him. Her heart leaped in her chest at the touch of his tongue on her lower lip. Gort coughed loudly and Aisling bumped her with her hip.

"Quit it you two, you want Sarie to catch you snogging in the hall?" Gort whispered loudly.

Coll drew back. Laurel experienced a sharp sense of loss, as if something important was missing as he withdrew. He kept hold of her hand and smiled at her. She smiled back and then bolted into her room at the sound of Sarie's voice at the foot of the stairs.

"Night, Laurel," Coll's voice came through the door.

She pressed her fingers to her lips and stared at the closed door. "Night, Coll," she whispered.

Aisling caught her hand and pulled her down on the bed. "What was that all about?" she demanded. "When did you and Coll get all intense and into copping off in the hall? C'mon, spill."

Laurel put her hands to her hot cheeks. "I have never in my whole life been kissed like that," she exclaimed. "Holy crap, I didn't even know you could feel like this. Is it like that when you and Gort are making out?"

"Is it like what?" Aisling tipped her head to the side and giggled.

"I don't know…like your mind blanks out and you just want to crawl into his skin to get closer to him…" she trailed off.

"Oh Laurel, you've got it bad." Aisling laughed. "It's nice when Gort and I snog, but so far the earth hasn't moved. He acts like he's afraid I'll break or something."

"Maybe you need to take the lead more," Laurel suggested, happy to have the conversation turn away from her feelings for Coll.

"Mmm, maybe." Aisling got into her nightie and slid under the covers.

Laurel got changed as well and turned out the light before getting into bed. In minutes Aisling's even breathing told her she was asleep. Laurel lay for a long time listening to the wind and reliving the incident at the top of the stairs.

Chapter Eighteen

The wind had dropped in the morning when Laurel woke up. She rolled over in bed and kneeled to look out the window. The sky still threatened rain, but only thick mist blanketed the house at the moment. Ash sat up beside her rubbing her eyes. “Is it still storming?”

“Seems to have stopped for now,” Laurel told her.

“Brill, we should be able to get our shopping done.” Aisling got out of bed and disappeared down the hall to the bathroom.

“The WC is clear if you want to use it before the boys get in there,” she said gaily when she re-entered the bedroom.

Laurel stepped out of bed and hopped down the hall, the floor freezing on her bare feet. Coll pounded on the door just as she finished washing up. She opened the door and slipped by him without meeting his gaze.

“Morning, Laurel,” he said as she passed.

“Morning,” she mumbled and fled to the safety of her room. In the cold light of day the intimacy of the night before was oddly embarrassing.

The girls dressed quickly in the early morning chill and went down to the kitchen to see about breakfast. Emily was already frying rashers of bacon at the Aga while Sarie scrambled eggs beside her.

“Set the table, would you girls?” Emily said over her shoulder.

“Are those slug a beds up yet?” Sarie asked.

“Do I smell bacon?” Gort asked as he preceded Coll into the room.

“My fav breakfast ever,” Coll enthused.

"So the plan is this. Emily will run the girls into town after breakfast and the chores are done and drop you off by the Wharfside Shopping Centre. You can find something on the high street if you don't find what you want there. I have some messages to run, but I'll drop Coll and Gort off at the house," Sarie outlined the plan.

"I need you boys to give the house a once over, please. Hoover the rugs, and sweep out the grates in the fireplaces. Tidy things up, you know the drill," Emily said.

"Sure, Gramma," Coll replied. "We know what to do. Do you want the sheets changed on the beds?"

"Only if they need it, but you could beat the rugs in the hall and by the door to the garden, if you would," she replied.

"No worries," Gort replied, speaking around a mouthful of bacon and toast.

Aisling smiled at him indulgently and Laurel just shook her head and applied herself to her own breakfast.

It was just past noon when Emily dropped them at the corner of Wharf Road across from the harbour. "Sarie or I will be back to pick you up by four, don't be late," she reminded them.

"We'll be here. Bye, Em," Ash called as the car pulled away. Linking her arm with Laurel, they watched the combers crash on the breakwater with a slapping boom.

She held the wind swept hair out of her face with one hand. "I could stand here all day listening to the waves make that sound. I never realized how strong the sea is or how tall the waves can actually get." Laurel remarked.

"We'd better get a move on if we want to meet Emily on time," Aisling said, pulling Laurel away from the harbour and toward the shops.

"You're right. Let's go spend some money." She laughed and dragged Ash over to look in the window of New Look at the clothes displayed there.

"We won't find anything for your folks in there," Ash advised her. "Maybe in The Dressing Room or Mash, up on Market Jew Street. Were you thinking of clothes for your mum?"

"I don't know." Laurel frowned. "Maybe I should look for something that will remind her of Penzance when we're back home. Is there a local craft shop or maybe an art gallery or something? I don't want anything too touristy. It'd be like buying a white cowboy hat when you come to Calgary. Lame."

Aisling thought for a minute. "There's the Glass House Gallery, they have stuff done by local artists, or there's the Morrab Studio further along at Alverton and Morrab. They're a gift shop with some nice things. Let's try the Glass House first, it closest."

Two hours later they were laden down with Laurel's purchases. She'd found a lovely ceramic bowl in shades of blue, turquoise and aqua for Sarie which she planned to add to the present she'd brought from home. They wandered in and out of some more shops and finally settled down at the Victorian Tea Room for a rest. Laurel leaned her chin on her hand with her elbow on the table and watched the people passing by.

"Whatcha thinking about?" Aisling nudged her with her foot.

"Nothing really, just people watching," she answered.

"Do you think your mom would let you come to visit me next summer?" The idea just popped into Laurel's head. "I hate that we live so far away from each other. You'd love Carly and you'd get to meet Chance. Let's just hope he's got himself a girlfriend by then."

"That would be super, but I don't know if Mum will go for it."

"Maybe she'll agree if she meets Mom and Dad while they're here," Laurel suggested.

"She might," Aisling agreed. "We'll have to wait and see, I guess."

The waitress brought the check and Laurel pulled some bills from her wallet. "Let me get it, Ash. My treat."

"Ta," Ash said. She leaned over and tipped her head toward the back of the shop where a blond haired waitress was delivering an order to a table there. "Recognize her?" she whispered.

"No, not really. Although she does look familiar." Laurel attempted to look in that direction without appearing to be looking.

Ash giggled at her. "It's Adelle, Stuart's sister."

"Really?" Laurel couldn't resist turning around for a better look at the girl who was chasing after Coll. "Huh, well I'm glad Coll isn't interested in her. Is Stuart still the miserable ass he was when I was here before?"

Aisling shook her head. "Believe it or not, he's working on a fishing boat out of Mousehole. He lives over there now. He cleared out once he got his O levels. Old man Pritch spoke up for him and got him a job on one of his mate's boats. I haven't seen Stuart in ages. We'll probably run into him tonight though, at the festival."

"Something to look forward to," Laurel remarked dryly and then giggled.

"He's actually been nice to me anytime our paths have crossed. Maybe getting out of the house has been good for him," Aisling said.

"I'm surprised he didn't want to be a cop like his dad." Laurel gathered up her parcels.

"I'm not. From what Emily's said after talking to Sam Pritchard, Stuart doesn't want to be like his da in any way. Him working on a fishing boat is a direct stab at Ted. He always spouts off about how fishermen fish 'cause they can't find anything better to do," Ash replied.

"That can't make him very popular in Newlyn or anywhere hereabouts." Laurel shook her head.

"That's very true, but Ted doesn't seem to care, just hides behind that badge of his." Aisling glanced at her watch. "We'd best get going or we'll miss our ride."

Laurel hurried along behind Ash wishing she hadn't bought quite so much stuff. "I can't believe that Mom and Dad will be here soon. I never thought he'd ever set foot in Penzance, or even England. They're on the train right now, maybe they've even crossed the Tamar at Plymouth and are actually in Cornwall already." She lengthened her step and drew even with her friend.

"What's he like, your da?"

"He likes to act like he's tough, but he's really a big marshmallow inside. Mom can usually get him to do whatever she wants. The only time he's ever held out on her was about Gramma Bella." She laughed as a thought suddenly occurred to her. "I bet he's wearing his hat, even on the train."

"Why is that so funny? Lots of men wear hats." Aisling looked up at her.

"Not western hats," Laurel chortled.

"You mean a cowboy hat, like in the movies?" Ash's eyes widened.

Laurel nodded, still chuckling. The wind picked up as they turned down New Town Lane. Ash glanced up at the sky.

"It looks like rain. I do hope it holds off for the festival tonight."

"Me, too. Although it's kind of nice to be out in the rain. Some years we don't get hardly any at home."

"Oh, look! There's Sarie, and the boys are with her." Aisling pointed with her free hand. "Gort, over here!"

Coll and Gort came to meet them and relieve them of some of the packages. Coll's hand lingered on hers as Laurel passed him the bags. Her face flamed with heat and she couldn't bring herself to look at him.

They hurried across the street and piled into the car. "We have just enough time to get home and put things to rights before we need to meet your folks at the station," Sarie announced.

"Do you think your da will like me?" Coll whispered in Laurel's ear.

The feathery touch of his breath sent shivers over her skin. "There's no reason he shouldn't…but he does seem to be pushing Chance at me all the time." She met Coll's gaze. "Besides, it doesn't really matter what he thinks, you're my friend and that's what counts." He reached for her hand and twined his fingers with hers, the worried look leaving his face.

"No canoodling back there," Sarie called from the front and Laurel jumped guiltily. She glanced sideways and smiled. Gort and Aisling were untangling themselves from each other, twin flags of red highlighting Gort's cheeks. Ash grinned and straightened her hair.

When they reached the farm, they made short work of the chores and putting things away. Laurel and Ash dashed upstairs to change the sheets on the bed in the spare room and put clean towels in the WC.

"Dad's gonna make a joke out of that, you know," Laurel said.

"Out of what?" Ash glanced over her shoulder.

"Calling the bathroom the WC for water closet. He'll start calling the outhouse by the barns the OH, just wait and see." She giggled.

"I think I'm gonna like your da," Ash decided.

Finished with the upstairs, they clattered down to the kitchen. The yeasty scent of baking greeted them along with the rush of hot air when they pushed through the door. Sarie was just lifting a batch of scones and saffron buns from the Aga.

"Mmmm, saffron buns." Laurel took a deep breath. "My fav."

"I thought we'd have a cream tea for your folks when they arrive and then after they get settled a bit it will be time to scoot over to Mousehole." Sarie set the baking sheet on the counter and transferred the buns to a cooling rack.

A swirl of cold air announced the boys' arrival from the outdoor chores. Coll carefully set the basket of eggs by the sink and washed his hands. Gort appeared a minute later from the mud room, drying his hands on a towel which he tossed to Coll.

"There won't be room for all of us to meet the train. Emily will be here soon and I'd like you boys to stay here and help her get things ready," Sarie declared.

Laurel smiled at the relieved look that crossed Coll's face. He really was nervous about meeting her dad. "Can Ash come?"

Sarie nodded. "Yes, as long as there isn't too much baggage to fit in the boot we should all fit."

Laurel controlled her impatience. The urge to see her parents surprised her. It wasn't like she'd been away for months or anything.

Finally, Sarie was manoeuvering down the lane. A light mist gathered on the windscreen so she was forced to turn on the wipers. The sun had long since vanished in the mist and cloud, the head lamps failing to offer more than a few feet of visibility. They pulled into the car park just as the First Great Western arrived at the platform. Laurel jumped out of the car, and without waiting for her companions, raced past the station house toward the blue and yellow train. She saw her dad first, stepping out of the First Class car and lifting down the bag in the doorway, Mom followed, pushing another suitcase which Dad deposited on the platform. Her mom jumped lightly down the last step and looked around.

"Daddy!" Laurel barrelled into him and he caught her around the waist, lifting her up and swinging her in large circles like he did when she was little.

"Well, princess. So this is the place you're so in love with?" He set her on her feet and shook the moisture from the brim of his Resitol. He kept one arm around her.

"Hey, Mom." She reached out and gripped her mother's hand. "I'm so glad you guys are here. I missed you like crazy."

"We missed you too, honey." She turned to smile at Sarie and Aisling as they approached a more sedate pace. "Sarie! It's so good to meet you in person. I feel like I know you after all the letters we've exchanged over the years." She enveloped the older woman in warm embrace. "And this must be Aisling." Anna smiled and extended her hand to Aisling. "I've heard so much about you, it's wonderful to put a face to a name. I hope you'll think about coming to visit next summer. The least we can do is return your hospitality to our girl here." She grinned at Laurel.

"It's nice to meet you, Mrs. Rowan." Aisling gravely put her hand in Anna's.

"Please call me Anna. Mrs. Rowan makes me sound so old."

Aisling blushed a bit, but smiled. "All right then, …Anna."

Laurel pulled her dad forward by the hand. "This is Ash, Aisling, Dad."

Colton removed his hat and tipped his head down. "Pleased to meet you, Aisling." He extended his huge paw of hand, which totally engulfed the girl's smaller one.

"It's very nice to meet you, Mr. Rowan," Aisling's voice was barely above a whisper.

"We don't stand on formalities much, just call me Colt." Dad smiled and his eyes crinkled merrily at the corners.

Laurel slid both arms around his waist and hugged him hard. "This is Sarie." Laurel kept his hand in one of hers and the other pulled Ash along with them.

"Colton, I'm happy to finally meet you. You have your mother's chin, did you know that?" Sarie held his gaze with her own.

Laurel stopped breathing at the mention of Gramma Bella and Dad's arm felt like steel under her fingers. *Please, please don't let him blow his stack. Why couldn't Sarie have waited to mention Gramma?* She caught the look her mother sent to her husband and Laurel's shoulders relaxed a little. That was Mom's "you best be on your good behavior or else" look.

"Nice to meet you as well, Sarie. Thank you for looking after our Laurel," he replied, ignoring the reference to Bella.

"Let's get out of this wet. We'll just run back to the house and drop off your gear and get some food into you. Then there's a festival to go to later on." Sarie took the handle of one of the bags and pushed it across the platform toward the car park. Laurel walked with her mom, pushing the other suitcase, her hand firmly enclosed in her mom's. Dad followed behind, beads of moisture dripping off the wide brim of his felt hat, three other smaller bags slung across his back and another in his hand.

"Can I take anything for you?" Ash offered shyly.

"Thank you, but no. I can manage." His smile flashed white in the shadow thrown by his hat.

Aisling politely walked beside him.

"So where are these two young hooligans I'm always hearing about?" Colt asked her.

"They're at the farm with Emily, that's Coll's gramma, waiting for us," Ash replied.

"So, do I have anything to worry about? The young'un behaves like a gentleman around my daughter, does he?"

Aisling was startled into glancing up at him. She relaxed and smiled when he winked at her.

"Dad! I heard that. Don't be looking for dirt on him before you've even met him," Laurel protested.

They stopped by the car and Sarie opened the boot. The two larger cases fitted in. "The rest will have to go with us," Sarie declared.

"You get in the front, Colt," Anna suggested. "There's more room for your long legs. I'll snuggle in the back with the girls." She ducked into the car and settled with an arm around each girl on either side of her.

Colt folded himself up into the passenger seat. "Makes me appreciate my pick up," he remarked, removing his hat and setting it on his knee. He crammed two of the smaller bags by his feet under his knees.

Sarie handed the other two to Laurel who put one between her feet and the other on her lap. She grinned as Sarie gunned the car out of the station and onto the coast road toward the roundabout at the A30. Dad reached out a hand and clutched the dashboard, the knuckles turning white as they neared the heavy traffic careening around the traffic circle. Laurel glanced over at Ash and grinned. Her mother ruffled her hair. "Don't give him a hard time, it's a big step him agreeing to come here," she whispered in her daughter's ear.

Laurel nodded, but couldn't keep from grinning at the way Dad leaned away from the oncoming traffic in the front seat.

Presently, the car bumped up the narrow lane toward the welcoming lights of Sarie's cottage. She reversed into the spot nearest the mud room door and parked. Emily came out to greet them before Laurel could get out of the car.

Coll and Gort hovered behind her. She kept an eye on Coll's face when her Dad unfolded himself from the front seat and straightened up. He looked even taller and more imposing with the added height of his hat which he put on as soon as he was free of the car. Coll's eyes widened and his Adam's apple bobbed as he swallowed a number of times. Gort came forward to take one of the small bags from Aisling and Coll hurried to do the same for Laurel.

Sarie opened the boot and Colt came around to lift the suitcases out. Anna swung her legs out of the vehicle and stretched as she stood up. A smile lit her face when her gaze landed on Coll. He ducked his head and rushed off into the house with one of the suitcases and a smaller bag slung across his shoulder.

Coll and Gort hauled all the bags up to the spare room and returned to the kitchen. Laurel introduced Emily to her parents and turned at the sound of their footsteps in the hall just before the door opened. "This is Coll," she pulled him forward, "and this is Gort. These are my parents, Colt and Anna Rowan," she announced. Behind her back she crossed her fingers that Dad wouldn't go all protective parent on her.

"Nice to meet you," Gort stepped forward after first glancing at Coll, who was staring at Laurel's dad like he expected him to explode at any second. Gort shook her dad's hand and turned to her mom. "I'm glad you came, you're even prettier than your pictures."

Her dad turned his burst of laughter into a cough and lowered his head for a moment to hide his face. He'd put his hat back on after greeting Emily. Aisling pushed Coll forward. He reluctantly approached Laurel's dad.

"Nice to meet you," he managed to get out and stuck out his hand.

"Same," Colt responded. "I don't bite, son. What stories has Laurel been telling you?"

"N-nothing, sir." For once it was Coll and not Gort who stuttered. "You're just a lot bigger than what I was expecting," he blurted out before he could stop himself.

"I'm very happy to meet you, Coll. Laurel has told me a lot about you." Anna came forward to save him from further embarrassment.

"Thank you, I'm happy to finally meet you too." Coll turned to her, an expression of relief on his face.

"Come and sit, the cream tea is ready," Emily announced.

"Oh, I can't wait to taste this. Laurel raved about the cream teas when she came home last time." Anna clapped her hands.

"It's got like a million calories, Mom. But it's so good you just don't care," Laurel said helping herself to a scone and slathering it with a thick layer of clotted cream and blackberry preserves.

"This is very good," Colton spoke around a mouthful of scone. "You were right, princess. There is nothing like this at home."

"Colt! Don't talk with your mouth full," Anna scolded her husband but her eyes danced with laughter.

Anna insisted in helping with the washing up while Sarie took Colt out to see the horses. They came back in just as the Laurel placed the last mug on the hook.

"The rain has stopped, it's just heavy mist now," Sarie announced. "We might want to take a mac with us, though."

Colt looked at Laurel and mouthed silently, "A what?"

"A mac, a mackintosh is a rain coat, Daddy." She giggled at the face he pulled.

"I'm jus' a poor old Alberty cow hand, missy. Cain't you jus' call it a slicker?" Colt dropped into the querulous old man persona he used to tease her with when she was little.

"Don't be silly, Dad." Inwardly, she was glad he was in such a good mood and ready to tease her.

"We'll have to take both vehicles, we won't all fit into one," Emily said.

"Where are we gonna park?" Laurel remembered the tiny narrow streets in Mousehole. She wondered how anyone managed to park there at all.

"Up by the old Penolva Quarry on the hill if there's room. Just before the lifeboat station. Or if we're too late to get a spot there, we'll have to park in Newlyn and walk up." Sarie glanced at the clock.

Laurel found herself in the back seat of Sarie's car with Coll. Her mom got into the front passenger seat. Dad squeezed into the front of Emily's car, with Aisling and Gort in the rear.

"I think Dad is hoping Emily drives slower than Sarie," Laurel remarked with a giggle.

"You know how he hates not being in control," Anna agreed. "It's killing him not to drive."

"Did you see him at the roundabout?" Laurel giggled.

"He was comical," her mom agreed. "But I wouldn't like to have to negotiate it, I have no idea what the rules are. How in heaven's name do you know when to go, or how to get off it?" Anna shook her head.

"Gramma's not quite as scary as Sarie to drive with," Coll ventured to comment.

Anna smiled at him kindly. "Colt was quite the mad man when he was younger, we used to go mud bogging and I'm still not sure how we stayed shiny side up."

"Mud bogging?" Coll looked at Laurel.

"It's kind of a sport, I guess. Chance and the boys like it well enough. They find a big mud hole and drive through it making as much splash as you can. Then you skid and spin the truck around. They count to see who can spin the most times around. I only went with him once," she glanced at her mom. "They were all drinking and Chance had a hard time driving home."

"Just as well you were only driving on the back roads. I spoke to his mother about that afterward. If he wants to drink underage, that's his problem. But I don't like him taking you to a tailgate party like that." Anna's lips thinned in annoyance.

"I never went again. Chance is…different when he drinks," she assured her mom.

"Most men are," she replied. "There's plenty of time for that when you're older." She eyed Coll over Laurel's head.

Sarie followed Emily through Penzance and along the Western Promenade where the waves slapped at the sea wall. They passed through Newlyn and up the hill toward the old quarry.

"Why, the sign says *Mousehole,* I thought you said we were going to Mouzel," Anna exclaimed as the head lamps illuminated the sign when they climbed a hill.

"That how it's pronounced, Mom. Don't ask me why," Laurel replied.

Sarie pulled up behind Emily, snugging the car up against the hill in the tiny layby. "You'll have to get the other side," she told Laurel. Once everyone scrambled out of the vehicles, they assembled on the shoulder of the road and Sarie and Emily led the way around a bend in the road. Coll and Laurel walked behind them, with Gort and Aisling following. Anna and Colt brought up the rear holding hands.

"Oh, isn't it beautiful!" Anna came up beside Laurel when the harbour came in view. "Even some of the boats have light displays. What a pretty pretty little village."

"Look, Mom. See the display that looks like a pie with fish heads? That's Star-Gazey Pie."

The lights shone from the shops lining the harbour and more twinkled on the hillside where the village clung to the side of the steep incline that rose above the sea.

"Isn't it spectacular, Colt?" Her mother's face shone in the reflected light.

"It is a mighty pretty sight," he agreed.

Laurel rolled her eyes when he leaned down and kissed her mom. "Ewww, get a room, you guys!" she teased them.

Chapter Nineteen

The area around the harbour was so crowded it was hard to find a place to stand. Sarie and Emily took Laurel's parents into the bar of the Ship Inn. Laurel and her friends climbed up on some pilings to look out over the crowd.

"Have you heard from Gwin? That stupid council meeting should be over by now," Laurel whispered in Aisling's ear.

"I haven't heard anything, but remember how time runs different there? Still, I thought we would have heard something by now." Worry furrowed Ash's forehead.

"No sense worrying about what we can't change," Gort said. "Here come your parents." He nodded toward the noise and lights of the Inn.

Anna handed around take out cups of coco, while the adults held dark glasses of Guinness. Colt made a face as he took a sip. "I think I'll try some of the local beer next, maybe one of those ones with the weird name. Maybe a Doom Bar or a Proper Job." He grinned at his wife.

Emily joined them. "I just talked to Elvira, they're almost ready to make the announcement."

"What announcement?" Anna wanted to know.

"They make a big announcement in the bar that the Starry-Gazey Pie is ready to be served," Sarie said. "Let's get in there so we get a chance at some of the first pieces." The adults shoved their way through the crowd and into the Ship Inn. Laurel and her friends stayed at their vantage point.

"They'll bring some for us," Coll assured Laurel.

A man emerged from the Ship Inn holding a huge pan over his head. A loud cheer went up from the crowd. From her vantage point Laurel got a good look at the massive browned crust, but her stomach flipped at the sight of the fish heads and tails sticking up out of the crust. Dead blank eyes staring upward.

"You aren't supposed to eat the fish, are you?" She swallowed, unable to pull her gaze away from the fish heads. "What kind are they, anyway?"

"They're pilchards. Tom Bawcock is supposed to have brought in seven kinds of fish for his Starry-Gazey Pie, but it's only made with pilchards now," Coll said.

"You don't have to eat the fish if you don't want to," Ash told her.

"See why they call it Star-Gazey Pie, though?" Coll leaned forward on his perch. "Just look at those poor buggers."

The man disappeared back into the building. Laurel wasn't sure she'd be able to get any bit of the pie past her lips. Ash jumped beside her and almost bumped Laurel off the piling. She swivelled around to see what happened.

Gwin Scawen sat on Ash's knee, clutching the pocket of her jacket to keep from falling. "Gwin, what happened?" she demanded.

"Good even to you, Mistress Laurel," the little man said formerly.

Laurel sighed and remembered her manners. "Hello, Gwin. How are you tonight?"

"It is fine, I am. Thanks for asking," he replied.

"Gwin has news for us," Aisling said.

Laurel found Coll's hand and gripped it tightly. *They have to have ruled in Vear's favour, they have to.* She willed the piskie to get on with it and tell them what the verdict was. He seemed more interested in arranging himself comfortably tucked inside Aisling's jacket.

"Are you ready, now?" Ash smiled indulgently as the piskie.

"Yes, Mistress Aisling, my flower. I am ready to relate my tale." He paused to clear his throat. "The Grand Council convened and heard the appeal which the Council of Alba put forward on Vear's behalf, as they agreed to. It was a long and tedious affair. The Council of Kernow wasn't happy at all, they weren't, with having their ruling brought into question. They argued long and loudly and I thought they had tipped the scales in their favour before the selkie even had a chance to speak. But then his turn came and he spoke most eloquently, so he did. He confessed to breaking with tradition and common sense and falling in love with a mortal. The Council of Kernow hissed with pleasure at that admission, they were ready to start celebrating right then and there, so they were. But the selkie continued, he brought up all the old bad blood between some of Kernow council members and himself. That set the Grand Council members to thinking, so it did. Then he called Morgawr, the sea serpent, to speak on his behalf. You know, Morgawr, he can be quite amusing when he sets his mind to it. He spun them quite a tale, told how he had just happened to be swimming and fishing near where the Council of Kernow were holding a secret meeting. Oh, they protested when they heard that, the Kernow members, but the Grand Council ruled they wanted to hear what he had to say. The sea serpent related how they'd conspired to blacken Vear's reputation and get him banished. They didn't like it one bit, that he consorted with the mortals and sometimes helped drive schools of fish toward the fishermen's nets when times were hard. By the time Morg was finished speaking I was feeling much more confident." The piskie paused and took a pull on a flask he produced from an inner pocket of his coat. "Tale telling is thirsty work. At any rate, I thought the hearing would end there and they'd hand down their decision. But no, then they called me forward. I wasn't expecting it, I wasn't. I can tell you my knees were fair knocking together, me speaking to the likes of the Grand Council. They asked me a lot of questions and I don't rightly recall what I said in return, but it must have been suitable because the selkie was smiling and nodding when I was allowed to step down."

"What did they decide?" Laurel couldn't bear the suspense a moment longer.

"Hist, now. Here come the big ones." Gwin whisked out of sight into the depths of Aisling's coat.

"Here you go, princess." Dad handed her a takeaway container with a goodly portion of pie on it. A fish's dead eye stared up at her.

"Thanks," she managed to say weakly.

Colt was holding his own plate gingerly and making no effort to sink his plastic fork into it. Anna was chewing carefully while Sarie and Emily dug into theirs enthusiastically. Coll, Gort, and Aisling were making good head way on their pieces. She noticed Ash sneaking bits into the front of her coat and Gwin's thin fingers snatching the crumbs. She caught her eye and giggled. Sarie glanced at Aisling and smiled. Laurel was sure Sarie knew exactly what was going on. Laurel decided she might as well cowboy up and try the pie. It wasn't likely she'd ever get another chance. Surprisingly, it wasn't as bad as she feared. If she just avoided looking the fish head in the eye and concentrated on the potatoes and egg it was actually pretty good. She grinned at Dad and silently challenged him to take a forkful. He grinned back and grimaced as he took a big bite. She giggled at the look on his face when the fish head in his piece fell against the side of the container.

Someone started singing the Tom Bawcock song she'd heard in Sarie's kitchen. She remembered some of the chorus and joined in. There was a lot of good hearted jostling and dancing in the middle of the crowd. Anna took Colt's hand and dragged him out into the heart of it. Emily wandered off to see if Elvira needed help in the kitchen as the pie was now being served in the restaurant as well as the bar of the Inn.

Gwin popped back out the moment they left. "As I was saying," he wiped some crumbs from his upper lip and smoothed the lapels of his tattered jacket, "The Kernow craytures called foul, but the Grand Council was having none of it. They went into a conclave and it took ever so long for them to conclude it. Bella was clinging to the selkie so tight if they'd wanted to separate them someone would have had to cut off her arm. The selkie he had his arm around her, daring any of the Council of Kernow to come near her. Oh, it was a grand sight, so it was."

"What happened? What did they decide?" Laurel couldn't contain herself any longer.

"Patience is a virtue, Mistress Laurel," Gwin chided her. "I'm coming to that, so I am. The Grand Council came back and they conferred with the Council of Alba and then met with the Council of Kernow for a bit. There were a lot of raised voices and shouting but it availed them nothing. Once the Grand Council has decided, nothing will sway them. The Kernow members had to stay and hear the decision whether they liked it or no. A lot of hissing and mumbling there was too. Then the Council Chief called Vear Du and Bella to come forward and hear the verdict. So they did, and they stood there bravely, so they did. The decision came down in Vear Du's favour, but there were some conditions attached to it. Vear pulled the Chief aside and they nattered for the longest time. Bella was fair beside herself standing there all alone with the Kernow contingent hissing at her. Then Morgawr went to her side and I did, too." He straightened his hat and pulled on his lapels. "Then the selkie came back and swung Bella around and around, laughing and kissing her. I came here to bring you the news straight away, so I did," he finished proudly.

"Where is Gramma Bella?" Laurel demanded. "Daddy's here and she should come and see him. I know I can make them see reason and make up. I just know it. But I have to get them together first." She smacked her fist on her thigh in frustration.

"Patience," Gwin reminded her. He stood on tiptoe balancing himself with a hand on Aisling's shoulder. "There," he pointed a long twiggy finger, "they come!"

Laurel whipped her head around so fast she fell off the piling. "Where is she?"

"I see a man who looks like Vear, but I can't see your gramma," Aisling reported.

"You'll see, oh you'll see, so you will," Gwin said.

The crowd swirled around and in a gap in the revelers Laurel glimpsed Vear Du with his arm around a woman with her back to Laurel. "Gramma Bella," she cried, starting to push through the crowd. "Gramma Bella!"

The crowd buffeted her from her course, but finally she reached the couple. "Gramma Bella," she threw her arms around the woman. "I'm so happy you're here!"

"Laurel, my pet," Bella turned and hugged her. "Gwin Scawen said you'd be here. I need to talk to you about something important."

"Hello, Laurel," Vear's voice was rich and deep, just like she remembered it. She hugged him too, inhaling the scent of tobacco overlaid with a faint odour of fish.

"Gwin said the council ruled in your favour, so you won. You can see Gramma whenever you want." Laurel let him go but kept an arm around him and one around Bella. "Daddy's here." She looked up at Bella. Her grandmother's face paled.

"He's here? With Anna?" she whispered.

Vear tipped his head down. "Colton is here? My son is here?" The selkie's voice broke on the last word.

"Yes, yes. Dad and Mom are both here. C'mon, we have to find them." She began to tow them along behind her as she bulldozed her way through the crowd.

"Laurel," Bella made her stop. "Don't get your hopes up. Your father may not want to see me at all. It's been a long time."

"Too long, if you ask me," Laurel insisted. "Look, there they are. Daddy!"

The tall man in the cowboy hat turned at the sound of her voice and started toward her, his large frame making a path for the blonde woman who followed behind. His pace slowed as he neared her and saw the couple standing with her.

"Daddy, look who's here." Laurel danced on her toes. "I found Gramma Bella." She thought it might be too soon to tell him who else was there.

"Mother," he tipped his head.

"Colton, I've missed you," Bella's voice broke and tears stood in her eyes. "I should have told you the truth right from the start, I should…"

“Daddy,” Laurel scolded him, “she’s your mom. You always say you shouldn’t hold a grudge, least that’s what you always tell me when I get mad.” She stamped her foot.

Anna pushed past her husband and gathered Bella in her arms. She hugged her mother-in-law and her daughter, and looked at her husband with a challenge in her eyes.

“I never stopped loving you, Colt,” Bella said.

Vear stepped forward before Laurel could stop him. “I think it is me you should be angry with and not your mother,” he began.

“Who are you?” Colt looked the man who equaled his height directly in the eye. “This is family business.”

“Family, yes. Well, you’ve got that part right. It was my moment of indiscretion that set all this in motion. I’m your father.”

Laurel hid her face in her mother’s shirt. This was all wrong. Dad and Gramma hadn’t had a chance to make up yet, and now Dad was gonna go ballistic. Her mother’s arm tightened around her.

“What kind of horseshit is this?” Colt demanded. “You’re not old enough to be my father. You’re younger than I am for God’s sake.”

“So it may appear. But I am and truly your sire. See the way your hair grows in a huge cowlick over your forehead. And you have a birthmark on your left hip that is shaped like a great seal. You carry my blood whether you like it or no. If you wish to mad at someone, be angry with me. I should have known better, I did know better. But I loved your mother, she wasn’t more than a child herself, and in danger of being shackled to a miserable excuse for a mortal. I love her still, I have never stopped.”

Laurel peeked at her father. His mouth opened and closed, but no sound came out. Anna stepped toward Vear Du and offered her hand. “I’m Laurel’s mother and Colton’s wife so I suppose that makes you my father-in-law.” She smiled and the selkie hugged her, keeping a wary eye on his son as he did so.

Anna released him and took Laurel's hand. "I think we should let your father and his parents have some time alone to come to terms with this. Let's go find your friends."

"But I need to stay. I can keep Daddy from flying off the handle, you know I can."

Her mother shook her head. "No, Laurel. I know you have good intentions, but this is something your father has to work out for himself. Colt," she laid a hand on his arm and he looked down at her with a bemused expression on his face, "why don't you three go somewhere quieter and talk this out?"

For a moment Laurel thought he was going to refuse. He looked at Vear and shook his head, but followed the pair out of the harbour area. Laurel saw them go into Pam's Pantry further down the beach. "I still think we should go with them," she insisted, pulling on her mother's arm.

Anna laid her hand over hers. "Laurel, you'll understand better when you're older. A proud stubborn man like your dad needs to do things in his own way in his own time. If we interfere he might never forgive Bella. I know he still loves his mother, but he's got a lot of anger too. And as for meeting his father," she shook her head and glanced toward where they'd disappeared, "that puts a whole new spin on things. This is something your dad needs to do on his own," she repeated.

"What happened? Where's your dad?" Coll asked when Laurel and her mom found them in the crowd in front of the Ship Inn.

"He's talking with Gramma Bella and Vear," she said unable to control the tremor in her voice.

"Oh, my." Emily put a hand to her throat.

"It's high time this nonsense between him and Bella was done with," Anna said with a hint of steel in her voice.

Sarie smiled at her over Laurel's head. "Anyone want something from the bar? I'm going in."

"I'll come with you." Anna took her arm from Laurel's shoulder. "You'll be okay with your friends?" She turned to follow Sarie, but then turned back. "Don't, under any circumstance, go looking for your father. Is that clear?"

Laurel nodded reluctantly. How did Mom know exactly what she was thinking? She'd planned to go find out what was going on as soon as she got the chance. Coll came beside her and slid his hand into hers. "Did he find out the selkie is his dad?"

"Oh yeah. Vear just blurted it out without any lead up or anything. He was trying to protect Gramma Bella, but still…"

"I don't know what I'd do if my da suddenly came back," Coll said. Laurel squeezed his hand and leaned her head on his shoulder.

"I wish mine would come back," Gort said quietly. "Sometimes I'd like for him to be here and other times I'd like to yell at him and tell what a scrote his brother was." Aisling stroked his cheek and he turned his head and kissed her palm.

"Is Gwin still with you?" Laurel had a sudden thought.

"I am here, Mistress Laurel." He popped out of Aisling's hair where it fell unbound over her shoulders.

"Can you go and find out what they're talking about? Dad and Vear, I mean. Or if they're talking at all. Dad might have asked him out behind the barn by now." Laurel chewed her bottom lip.

Coll looked down at her in puzzlement. "There's no barn around here."

"It just means he wants to settle things with his fists," Laurel explained.

"Oh, that would not be good." Gwin shook his head. "The big black one is ever so strong."

"So is my dad, and he's really tough when he's mad," Laurel argued.

"Why don't you just go and see what you can see?" Aisling suggested.

"Of course, my flower. For you, anything." The piskie stood up and then popped out of sight.

"Let's just hope he doesn't get so entertained he forgets to come back and tell us what he knows." Aisling sighed.

"He is rather unreliable," Gort observed.

"But very useful too," Aisling defended her friend.

The crowds were thinning a bit and they moved closer to the stone building and leaned near the door to the bar. Anna and Sarie emerged with Emily in tow. Laurel took the cup of hot chocolate from her mom and wrapped her cold hands around it.

"No sign of them yet?" Anna asked.

Laurel shook her head.

"It all goes well," Gwin Scawen materialized on Aisling's shoulder. "Oh, my!"

"Hello, Gwin, you scamp," Sarie greeted him before he could wink out again.

"Greetings, Mistress Sarie. Well met." He hopped down to the cobbles and bowed low. "And to you, Mistress Emily." He sidled over to stand by Anna's feet. "Welcome to Kernow, Laurel's mother," he said. He bowed so low his nose touched the ground.

"Hello, Gwin Scawen. I want to thank you for helping Laurel when she needed it. I am in your debt."

"Oh, no. Mistress Anna, 'twas my pleasure, so it was. It is not often one such as I get to see the king of the faeries brought to heel as neatly as you did that day under the Tor."

"Yes, well, that's all still a bit of blur, although Laurel has told me what happened." Anna looked slightly uncomfortable. "But tell me, you went and spied on Colt and his parents?"

"Now, Mistress Anna, spy is such a nasty word. Let us just say I popped in to see how things were progressing."

"Fine, let's say that then." Anna raised an eyebrow at the piskie.

"There is no blood shed which is a fine thing. And no one has…what did you say, Mistress Laurel…gone out behind the barn. So things are progressing nicely. Bella is crying, but they are happy tears. The son is scowling, but he is listening to what the big black one is saying. That is all I know.

"Well, it's something. At least Colt hasn't stormed out of there yet." Anna smiled at Laurel.

"Look, there's Bella." Sarie waved to attract her attention.

She joined them, her eyes a bit red rimmed but she was smiling. Bella gathered Anna and Laurel in a hug. "He says he understands a bit better now and he forgives me," she reported.

"Where is Colt?" Anna searched the crowd with her eyes.

"I left him and Vear talking. There are somethings that they need to settle between them that don't require my presence apparently," she said.

"Is that wise?" Anna looked worried.

"I think that if there was going to be any fireworks it would have already happened," Bella replied. "But there is something I need to talk to you and Laurel about. Afterward, I need to speak with you, Sarie."

"Okay." Anna drew Laurel and Bella away out of the lights and merriment around the inn. She stopped by the narrow entrance to Duck Street. Bella glanced around to be sure they were alone.

"Anna, thank you so much for getting Colton to come here. I feel we have finally begun to mend the rift between us. But that makes what I have to tell you all the more bittersweet."

"What do you mean?" Anna asked, taking Laurel's hand.

"As you know from Gwin, the Council ruled in our favour. So Vear and I can see each other as often as we wish. But without my knowledge, he made another bargain. One I'm not sure I approve of. It is weighted much more in my favour than in his."

"What is it?" Laurel asked.

"It seems the great idiot has traded his immortality in exchange for a lengthening of my life," she confessed. "By the time I knew of it, it was already done."

"But what does that mean?" Laurel asked. It didn't make sense to her at all.

"It means that sometime in the far away future Vear Du will fade away, in effect, he will die. I will also die, but many many years after I should."

"What's so bad about that? You get to be together, there'll be lots of time for you and Dad to make up for all that lost time…" Laurel stopped at the look on Gramma Bella's face.

"It's not so simple. In order for me to have long life, we must live in the other worlds most of the time. Vear says I will actually get younger for the first few centuries."

"Centuries?" Anna breathed the word, an astounded expression in her eyes.

Bella nodded. "In appearance I'll go back to the girl I was when I first met him, all those years ago. But I will keep all my memories. As you know, Laurel, Vear doesn't look much older than his early twenties, even now. But I won't be able to be part of your life, to watch you grow up and see my great grandbabies. Only if you come to Cornwall and call to us using the talisman he gave you will I be able to see you."

"I'll tell my kids, and they can tell their kids so we'll never forget you and you'll get to know the future generations of our family," Laurel said fiercely. "I'll pass the talisman down from me to my kids and explain why it's so important they do the same."

"That might work, Laurel. At least it gives me hope. I do miss you terribly, but my heart has always belonged to Vear Du."

"Is Dad okay with all this?"

"He's trying to understand. I have left my house in Bragg Creek to you in your father's trust until you're old enough to decide if you want to live there or sell it. Vear is arranging things so there will be money transferred to cover the taxes and the costs for maintenance, with some over to make life easier for you and Colt, Anna, and some to put in a trust fund for you, Laurel."

"I don't want you to leave, Gramma. I just found you again." Laurel threw her arms around Bella and buried her face in her shoulder.

"I don't want to either, but the die is cast, so to speak. This is what I needed to tell you. But for tonight let's enjoy the fun and each other's company. Tomorrow is time enough for sadness," Bella suggested.

"I wish I had your ability to just live in the moment," Anna said to her mother-in-law.

"It's something I learned so I wouldn't throw myself off the bluff into the Old Man River," Bella said with a touch of bitterness in her voice. "I was so terribly homesick for the longest time when I left here."

"Let's go see if your father is finished talking with Vear Du," Anna said. She took Laurel's hand and led her back toward the harbour. Bella walked at her other side.

When they found the others Colt and Vear were still missing. Bella and Sarie went off to speak privately. Laurel wondered how Sarie would take the news. She'd been a part of the story since the beginning and now it seemed their paths were really going in different directions. She managed to fill her friends in on what Gramma Bella told her without crying. She leaned on Coll for support and he snugged his arm around her shoulders.

"That's some bargain he made," Aisling said. "He must love your gramma a whole lot."

"I can't believe he gave up his immortality for her," Gort looked over at the woman talking to Sarie, the light making a halo around her head.

"Oh, look. Here comes Dad."

Laurel turned to tell her mom, but Anna was already making her way toward her husband. The tall man wrapped his arms around her as if she was the most precious thing on earth. Laurel was surprised and alarmed to see his shoulders shake with sobs. Anna stroked his head and kissed his ear. Laurel shrugged out of Coll's embrace with a quiet apology and hurried over to her parents. She put her arms around her dad and hugged as hard as she could. "It's gonna be okay, Dad." She repeated over and over. Finally, her dad stroked her hair and kneeled down to hug her.

"Yes, it will be okay, princess. You're right." He wiped his eyes with the back of his hand and took Anna's hand with the other. With his wife and daughter on either side they went back to join Laurel's friends who were just filling Emily in on the news.

Vear Du loomed up out of the crowd behind her dad. Laurel tried to smile but the pain in her chest just made her mouth twist. The selkie put his hand on Colt's shoulder and he turned to greet him.

"It is time we were going, but I couldn't leave without speaking with you once more." He extended his hand and Colt took it. The two men held each other's gaze and Laurel saw them tremble as they gripped their hands together. Finally, Vear pulled her dad into a bear hug and they hung on so long she began to wonder if they'd ever let go. Mom stood beside her with tears running down her cheeks. Finally Vear stepped back and Colton held his arms out to his mother. With an inarticulate cry, Bella gathered him in her arms. Laurel fought back the tears and Gort sniffed loudly behind her. Coll put his hand on her shoulder for support and she covered it with her own. Suddenly, Vear was in front of her. He bent down to her level and gazed at her face. "I think I will miss you most of all. So young and so brave. I would expect nothing else from my granddaughter. You also have a gift from me. Because of the blood that runs in your veins, you can never drown, no matter how rough the water. And you will live a long and healthy life, far longer than an ordinary mortal, for there is nothing ordinary about you." He hugged her. Laurel tried to say something but her voice was drowned in her tears. "I know what's in your heart, dear one. There is no need of words between us."

He stood up and turned to where Bella still clung to Colt. "Come, my beautiful Bella. There is time for one last dance and song and then we must be going. Say your farewells for now. It is never goodbye between those who love as we do."

He led her away into the crowd. Vear threw his head back and bellowed the words. A few villagers obviously knew him, but addressed him as Douglas.

"Why are they calling him by a different name?" Laurel asked Sarie, never taking her eyes off the couple.

"It's a name he uses when he walks the fields of mortals," she answered wiping a tear from her cheek.

"He's ever so clever, so he is." Gwin Scawen spoke from Aisling's shoulder. "Douglas comes from Dubh Glas, which is dark or black water in the Gaelic. What better name for a selkie?"

Laurel nodded. Her gaze met Gramma Bella's across the crowded square and she smiled. Vear tipped his dark head to her and led Bella in a series of intricate steps that took them to edge of the light.

"Go gently," Laurel whispered, and raised her hand with the forefinger crooked to call down a blessing from heaven in a gesture she remembered learning from Gramma Bella in her childhood.

"Go gently," her dad echoed from beside her.

The End

More Books by this author from Books We Love

Laurel's Quest (The Cornwall Adventures Book 1)

A Step Beyond (The Cornwall Adventures Book 2)

Storm's Refuge (A Longview Romance Book 1)

Historical Horror
By N.M. Bell

No Absolution

About the Author

Nancy M Bell has publishing credits in poetry, fiction and non-fiction. Nancy has presented at the Surrey International Writers Conference and the Writers Guild of Alberta Conference. She loves writing fiction and poetry and following wherever her muse takes her.

Please visit her webpage http://www.nancymbell.ca
You can find her on Facebook at
http://facebook.com/NancyMBell
Follow on twitter: @emilypikkasso

Books We Love, Ltd